D1531259

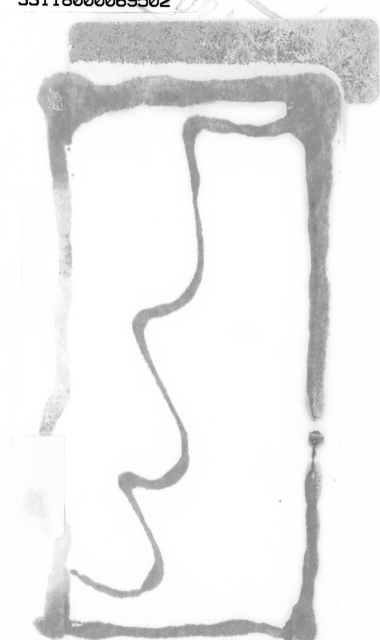

My Name Is
Sus5an Smith.
The 5 Is Silent.

My Name Is
Sus5an Smith.
The 5 Is Silent.

Louise Plummer

Delacorte
Press

Published by
Delacorte Press
Bantam Doubleday Dell Publishing Group, Inc.
666 Fifth Avenue
New York, New York 10103

Library of Congress Cataloging in Publication Data

Plummer, Louise.
    My name is Sus5an Smith. The 5 is silent. / by Louise Plummer.
        p.   cm.
    Summary: After years spent idolizing and championing her long-absent
and much-reviled Uncle Willy, seventeen-year-old Susan, a promising artist,
meets him by chance in Boston, where she is spending the summer, and
determines, against all advice, to prove her irrevocable love and devotion.
    ISBN 0-385-30043-3
    [1. Self-perception—Fiction.   2. Artists—Fiction.   3. Uncles—Fic-
tion.]   I. Title.
PZ7.P734My   1991
[Fic]—dc20   90-3765
                                                           CIP
                                                            AC

Designed by GDS/Jeffrey L. Ward

Manufactured in the United States of America

June 1991

10 9 8 7 6 5 4 3

BVG

52,696

For Tom

※

Springville, Utah 84663

※

∞ 1 ∞

On the same day that Uncle Willy deserted both Aunt Marianne and the United States Air Force, he spun me around at arm's length, grasping tightly to one ankle and one wrist. I was seven then, but I remember every detail of that afternoon as if it happened five minutes ago. My body swayed through the hot August air, and the sandal on my free foot flew off and hit the trunk of the cherry tree in our backyard. "Faster, faster," I cried, but Uncle Willy, panting, stopped and lowered me to the grass, still clutching my limbs.

"Girl, you wear me out," he laughed. He wiped the sweat from his forehead with the sleeve of his shirt.

"Susan, let Willy alone now," Mother cried from the brick patio next to the house. She and Aunt Marianne sat in canvas chairs watching us.

Uncle Willy let go of my ankle. I stood up quickly and grasped him around the waist. "Let me fly one more time," I pleaded with him, pulling on his thick black belt. "Just one more. Oh, pretty please."

"Susan, that's enough now." Mother sat up straight, shaded her eyes with one hand, and clasped the arm of her chair firmly with the other. "Go in the house now and stop bothering Willy. He doesn't want to spend his whole leave flying you around this back-yard. Go in and make us some Hawaiian Punch or something." She was pregnant then, and she smoothed her maternity dress over her large abdomen where Derek, my brother-to-be, was stored until it was time to come out.

"Maybe later?" I squinted at Willy.

"For sure, Ace." He laughed. He had the straightest, whitest teeth.

"I'm going to be a pilot, too, when I grow up, so I can go lots of places and see everything there is to see," I said, slipping into the flyaway sandal. I stretched my arms out, made motor noises with my mouth, and scurried around the cherry tree several times. "I want to go to Calcutta and Kuala Lumpur," I yelled.

Uncle Willy sat on the grass and watched me, smiling. I thought even then that he liked me a lot.

"Kuala Lumpur? Did she make that up?" Mother asked. She sat back in her chair again and fanned herself with the magazine that had lain in her lap.

"No, there's such a place. I've been there." Uncle Willy swatted silently at a flying insect. "It's in Malaysia."

"I've been there too. It sure is a long way from here—from home," Aunt Marianne sighed. She and Uncle Willy exchanged a quick glance and looked away from each other.

"I want to fly right over the mountains and away from here. I want to see the ocean and palm trees and lemon trees and have an armadillo for a pet," I said.

"An armadillo!" Mother gasped. "That's what we need all right —armadillo doo-doos all over the carpet."

Aunt Marianne laughed.

Uncle Willy said, "I'll send you an armadillo, girl, as soon as I find one."

"Would you? Would you really?" I clung to his waist again.

"Don't make promises you can't keep." Aunt Marianne's face was a warning.

"Susan, what about that Hawaiian Punch?" Mother shifted uncomfortably in her chair.

"We've got to be going," Willy said. He looked at Marianne, who was staring into her lap. "I'll go say g'bye to Russ over at the store and then I'll come back for you." He stood behind Aunt Marianne's chair. He touched her hair with his fingertips. "Okay?" he asked her.

"Fine." She spoke so softly, her head still bowed over her lap, I could barely hear her.

It occurred to me, watching Marianne's bowed head, that Willy and Marianne were fighting the way Mother and Dad did sometimes, not with shouting, but with long silences. Was that why he left?

"Wait," I said, following him to the back door. "I have a present for you."

Mother twisted around in her chair. "He'll be back in a few minutes, Susan. Give it to him when he comes back."

"It's okay." Uncle Willy waved his hand at Mother. "Okay, girl, get this great present, and then I'm going to say good-bye to your dad." He followed me through the kitchen and down the hall to my bedroom.

Crouching on the floor, I pulled the picture I had painted for him from under my bed. It was rolled up carefully and tied with red curling ribbon. I handed it shyly to Uncle Willy. "It's the best one I've ever done," I said.

He pushed the ribbon down the paper. It was a picture of him flying over the mountains in a small open airplane, the scarf around his neck blowing straight back into the wind, the pale blue sky spotted with tufts of white, scalloped clouds. Below, the landscape was dotted with tiny fir trees.

Uncle Willy stared at it. I mean, he was really looking at it, not the way Mother or Daddy looked at my drawings, barely glancing at them and laying them aside with only the barest comment,

"That's real nice, honey. How about your arithmetic? Have you done your arithmetic yet?"

"Girl, you sure can paint," he breathed.

"I'm the best artist in second grade," I said.

"This picture looks just the way I feel when I'm flying. The feeling is just right. How'd you do that?" he asked.

"I just tried to imagine what it would be like to fly over the mountains. I want to fly over them more than anything and see wonderful places," I said. I half hoped he would offer to fly me over that very day. Sometimes I dreamed that my parents contracted a light case of leprosy and had to give me up, and Uncle Willy and Aunt Marianne adopted me and let me travel with them all over the world.

"Kuala Lumpur." He smiled. He had a faraway look in his eyes.

I nodded. "And Sydney, Australia." I liked the ess sounds especially in Sydney, Australia.

"The mountains here are pretty splendid," Willy sighed. "Maybe a little claustrophobic. Listen girl," he said, holding me around the waist. His arms were brown and smooth, his fingers long and nicely shaped: artistic fingers. "When you do fly over the mountains, make sure you fly in your own plane so no one else can tell you where it is you have to go. Remember that. Fly in your own plane. It's real important."

I didn't know exactly what he was talking about, but I liked it when he kissed me on the cheek. I liked the way Uncle Willy smelled.

"Gotta go now." He rolled my picture back up and replaced the curled ribbon carefully, which I took to be a sign that he valued my gift. "Thanks for this." He clutched the painting in his fist. "I'll hang it above my bed and it'll remind me of you."

I followed him through the living room, taking two steps to his one to keep up with him. He kissed me again at the front door and then leapt off the front porch and got into his car, which was filled with boxes of wedding presents that he and Marianne hadn't had room for after their wedding. He honked the horn as he backed out of the driveway. I waved at him from behind the screen door. The tires screeched as the car lunged forward in the opposite direction of Daddy's store. He never came back.

That was when Aunt Marianne started living with us. I remember, because it was just before Derek was born. She jumped when the phone rang and answered it expectantly as if it might be him— Uncle Willy. Although she made no plans to go anywhere, she wore her best clothes and high heels. She primped her hair like a girl waiting for her first date. Her whole day was organized around the mailman's delivery time of two o'clock in the afternoon. Even after she enrolled in the beauty school in Provo, she would call Mother right after two to see if she'd received any mail. She didn't say "from Willy," but we all knew that he was the only one she wanted to hear from. He never even sent her a card.

I was the one who received a package on my eighth birthday, shortly after Derek was born. It was on Saturday, and Aunt Marianne had the afternoon off from the beauty school. She walked out to the street when she saw the mailman's truck. We could tell, Mother and I, just from looking at the way Aunt Marianne walked back up the driveway alongside our house, that there was something from Uncle Willy, although Marianne wasn't smiling.

Mother held the baby over her shoulder. "Now what?" she whispered under her breath. I held on to the new Barbie doll I had gotten for my birthday that morning.

"It's something for Susan," Aunt Marianne said, standing at the bottom of the porch steps. She waved the package weakly. "It's from Willy."

Mother pushed the screen door open and waited for Aunt Marianne to come in. "For Susan? Are you sure?"

She pointed at my name and handed me the package. She looked devastated.

"It's just because it's my birthday," I said.

"It's all right honey," she said. "Open it and see what he got you."

It was one of those spongy book mailing bags, stapled together at one end. Uncle Willy's name was written in ink in the corner, but there was no return address. Aunt Marianne held my Barbie doll while I worked open the staples. Inside the bag was a small white box with "Neiman-Marcus" printed on it in gold letters, and inside the box between two layers of pressed cotton was a thin silver chain looped through a perfect silver armadillo and a note scrawled in Uncle Willy's handwriting: "I promised you an armadillo. Happy Birthday. W."

I held the delicate necklace in my hand. I loved it beyond belief, but I didn't dare say anything in front of Marianne, who was obviously hurt.

"What is he thinking?" Mother asked. She was patting the baby vigorously on the back even though it was asleep. "That's an expensive necklace."

"Yes, Willy has good taste," Aunt Marianne agreed.

"I think you should have it," Mother said to her.

My fingers closed over the necklace and I stepped back. It was the most beautiful thing I'd ever owned.

"Absolutely not," Aunt Marianne said. "He sent it to Susan and she should have it."

"He left you nothing." Mother was indignant. "Susan is an eight-year-old girl. What does she need a necklace like that for?"

Aunt Marianne turned to me. "Do you want me to put it on for you?" she asked.

I looked up at Mother for permission. She searched Aunt Marianne's face and then just shrugged her shoulders.

Aunt Marianne fastened the silver thread around my neck. I felt the armadillo with my fingers.

"Don't break it," Mother said. "That little silver chain will be broken in twenty minutes."

"I won't break it," I said.

"It looks real cute on you," Aunt Marianne said. "Go look in the mirror." She sat on the piano bench, her arms folded tightly in front of her.

I ran into the bathroom.

"He stole all of your Francis I and then gives *her* a silver necklace. I think he's the biggest jerk in the world." I could hear Mother talking in the living room. Whenever Mother wanted to emphasize Uncle Willy's evil nature, she brought up the sterling-silver flatware, Francis I. She hissed when she said it. The silverware and the Royal Doulton china had been packed in the car on the day he took off. "Do you know how much one place setting of that costs nowadays?"

I looked so beautiful in the necklace. I couldn't even feel very sorry about some silly old forks and spoons.

"You can be sure it's all pawned now." Aunt Marianne's voice sounded weak.

"He's a total and complete jerk."

"I'm afraid you're right," Marianne said, and she burst out crying. I stayed in the bathroom but opened the medicine cabinet door so that I could see Aunt Marianne reflected in the mirror. I had never seen an adult cry before.

After that Aunt Marianne changed her name back to Schroeder and had the diamonds in her wedding ring made into a dinner ring, a term that didn't make a whole lot of sense to me at the time, because she wore the ring all the time and not just at dinner. She no longer waited for the mailman or called my mother in the afternoon unless she just wanted to chat. She had some money of her own and asked my parents if she could rent our basement, which was unfinished at the time. My parents could use any extra money they could get, so they were happy with the idea. Aunt Marianne had the basement finished into a small apartment for herself and a beauty salon in the front. She had an outside door put in at the side of the house that led into a small vestibule with two doors, one leading to the salon, one to her apartment. Sometimes she dated some of the guys around Springville and Provo, but she always said no to the really handsome ones. She didn't trust them, she said.

After that Uncle Willy's name was only spoken in whispers in our family, but I wore the armadillo necklace like a talisman to conjure up a vision of him, youthful, handsome, adventurous, artistic. I wore that necklace ten years and never broke the silver chain like Mother said I would. And Willy grew in my mind, godlike, with magical powers to make me fly through the air, soar like a bird right over the peaks of the Rocky Mountains. I never stopped loving Willy.

❧ 2 ❧

When Uncle Willy left, I was Susan Smith. Now, ten years later, I am *Sus5an* Smith. The 5 is silent. It's a silence that drives certain members of my family up the wall, but I figure if you're going to have the last name of Smith, then your first name should be more exotic than Susan or Sue or even Sioux. It should be Constantinople or September or interrupted with a number. My best friend has a great name, a name that makes heads perk up—Fiona McCafferty. I've known her since second grade and she's always been the only Fiona in the class—in the school even. On the other hand she knows *three* Susan Smiths. "But you're the only one," she tells me, "who spells it with a five," which is why I do it—to distinguish myself. I'm an artist and I choose to have a five in my name. Last year my work was photographed and printed in the *Salt Lake Tribune,* and even they printed my name with the silent 5, the way I asked them to. Fiona says I'm a powerful person without the 5. She can see it in my aura, she says.

Actually my full name is Susan Schroeder Smith, which sounds just like one of those grade-school tongue twisters: six singing, slimy snakes slowly sliding southward. My mother named me after her older sister, Susan Elizabeth Schroeder, who has never used the name Susan or Sue but goes by Libby. She would rather go by a canned-vegetable label than the name Susan. She lives in Boston, Massachusetts—as far from Springville, Utah, as she can get without getting wet. If Mother had had another daughter instead of my brother, Derriere (long for Derek, because he has this cute little tight tush), she would have named her after Aunt Marianne. She's the one who placed the sign in the front basement window: HAIR-STYLING BY MARIANNE. I don't like the sign. Signs like that don't belong in a residential neighborhood. They clutter the landscape. I may have borrowed that phrase from Mr. Tuttle, my studio arts teacher at the high school. He's always saying stuff like that. I personally, though, wouldn't have a commercial sign on my private home, but then I don't intend to have the kind of life my mother and father have had.

My dad, Russell Smith, owns a grocery store called Russell's Market, which is a cross between Allen's—this huge supermarket on Main Street—and a 7-Eleven, and doesn't make a whole lot of money. He always brings home all the wilted vegetables, like carrots grown limp, their ends curled under. My mother feeds us all that wilted junk, usually in some kind of casserole, the veggies overcooked and mixed with Campbell's cream of mushroom soup. I'm not going to eat another cooked-vegetable casserole when I leave home.

Anyway, because of the store my dad is rarely home except on Sundays, when the store is closed, and then he goes to church with us, eats a big dinner, and naps the rest of the afternoon. During the week he comes home for dinner and stays long enough to watch *Wheel of Fortune* and then returns to work until about ten o'clock. When he's not too tired, he will do his Vanna White imitation.

We were begging him to do it the night Derriere and I discovered Marianne with Heber McIntyre:

"Do it, Dad! You haven't done it for ages," Derriere begged.

"Speak, Vanna, speak!" I said.

Daddy and Mother still sat at the table, which hadn't been

cleared of supper dishes yet, talking softly to each other. His hand covered hers. I could tell that she didn't want him to go back to the store. I sat on the sofa, sketching in my notebook. The TV blared several commercials while we waited.

"Dad, come on, do Vanna White." Derriere was beginning to whine. One of his front teeth was chipped. He's kind of hyper and is always knocking into things. He shook the back of Daddy's chair.

"Don't do that," Mother ordered.

"Tell Daddy to do Vanna White, then." Derriere jumped up and down repeating, "Tell him, tell him." Mother covered her eyes with her free hand for a few seconds.

Daddy kissed her hand and slowly stood up. On the TV the *Wheel of Fortune* audience yelled in unison, "Wheel—of—Fortune!" and clapped their heads off.

Daddy raised his arms above his head and turned slowly around, grinning broadly at us. He walked to the light switch, clicked it on and off several times, bowed, and then clapped for himself.

Derriere screeched with laughter. I giggled and Mother smiled. On the TV Pat Sajak and the real Vanna White stepped out in front of the camera. She wore a red sequined jumpsuit, her lacquered mouth forming a perfect smile. The audience went crazy.

"Her teeth are so obviously capped," Mother said staring. "They look like a picket fence. I don't think she's that good-looking myself."

Daddy stood next to the TV, arms raised above his head, still grinning falsely. "I haven't got it quite right," he said through his teeth and glancing back at Vanna. "I'll be back in a minute." He minced out of the room and was gone several minutes.

"What's he doing?" Derriere asked. "Is he coming back? Where is he? Huh?"

"Derek, I don't know. Wait and see," Mother said.

Daddy stuck his head in the door. "Announce me, Derek," he ordered.

Derriere yelled above the noise of the television, "And now, here's our own Vanna White!"

Daddy strutted in, his arms up again, a smile pasted from ear to ear. Slowly he revolved around. We all burst out laughing. He had cut a huge hole out of the back of his shirt. There was only startling white skin and a sprinkling of moles.

"Her dresses are always backless," he said, maintaining the phony smile. He clapped for himself.

"That was a perfectly good shirt," Mother said. She was smiling, though.

"It was an old shirt," he said, sitting down next to her again.

"All of your shirts are old shirts," I said. "You should get some new ones."

"You can buy them with your money," Mother said. The smile was fading from her lips. Mother doesn't like to be reminded that we don't have any money.

"Does that tickle?" Derriere scrambled his hands through the hole in Daddy's shirt.

"Yes, it does," Daddy said. He turned and pulled Derriere off his feet and tickled him under his arms until Derriere got the hiccups.

"How about that? Does that tickle?" Dad stood up with Derriere on his shoulders.

"I'm tallest," Derriere sang. "I'm fifty feet taller than Susan."

"Big deal," I said quietly.

The contestant who was working on a "person" on *Wheel of Fortune* must have had the IQ of a sugarbeet. Everyone in the world knew it was "Greek Philosophers" except him. "I guess I have to spin," he said.

"I guess I'd better go," Daddy said. He put on his white coat over his shirt. His name, "Russ," was embroidered over the front pocket in blue. He turned. "Does the hole show through the material?"

Mother smiled. "Only the moles," she said.

"Don't go yet," Derriere pleaded. He was hanging on to Daddy's legs.

The guy on the TV spun "Bankrupt" and was put out of his misery. The lady next to him guessed "Greek Philosophers," but she only had $300, which is a big joke on a show where you can win $25,000 in one fell swoop.

Daddy kissed Mother's mouth. "See you later," he said. "Come and walk me out to the car," he said to Derriere, who continued to hang on his legs. Daddy used to horse around with me like that—you know, letting me hang on his legs—and he used to let me touch the ceiling and he'd say, "So high. Susan can go so high." I miss that kind of stuff sometimes. Now he leaned down and patted my cheek with his hand. "See you later, beautiful."

"See you later, Vanna," I said. I blew him a kiss.

Mother began clearing the table. "Come and fill up the dishwasher," she said.

"In a minute," I said. "Let me finish my drawing." I had drawn Daddy strutting around the kitchen. It was a good likeness.

"The drawing will have to wait until after you've done your work," Mother said.

"Drawing *is* my work," I insisted, but I put my notebook down and walked to the dishwasher. "I hate dishes," I muttered.

"I imagine that even artists do dishes," Mother said. She watched me briefly. "Susan, for heaven's sake, *rinse* the dishes before sticking them into the dishwasher. Look at this plate! It has half of tonight's dinner left on it. You can't put this in there like that. It'll clog up the machine." Her face had a pinched quality.

On *Wheel of Fortune* the contestant who couldn't guess "Greek Philosophers" ended up winning a bundle, because he landed on the $5,000 spot on the wheel and asked for an *S,* and there were four of them for *Mississippi Riverboat.* Then he won a $30,000 sports car in the bonus round.

I rinsed the plate and wished Mother would leave the room so that I could just dump the plates, gunk and all, into the dishwasher and be done with it. What's the point of having a dish-washer if you have to rinse the dishes first? She was always hover-ing about, making sure that everything was perfect.

The guy on television was sitting in his sports car and waving like a crazy man from the front window, his fat wife seated next to him. They looked ridiculous in that sports car. They should have given him a cattle truck or something. "I wish I owned a car like that," I said.

Mother was taking all the spices out of the spice cupboard and wiping down the shelves. "What would you do with it?" she asked.

I looked out the back window and watched Derriere playing with his trucks in the sandpile. Above the trees the Rocky Moun-tains blotted out the horizon.

"I'd drive over the mountains and straight out of here. I'd go all the way to Boston and live with Aunt Libby," I said. "Then I'd sell the car and be an artist. I'd never come back."

Mother sighed.

It's true. I wouldn't live in Springville, Utah, also known as Art City because of the museum here, if I had any choice about it. The "art" in Art City isn't that noticeable when you're driving along Main Street. It's so clogged with gas stations, restaurants, all of them claiming home cooking, roller-skating rinks, and ugly storefronts connected by a crisscrossing of electrical power lines that I think Garbage Can Art City might be a better name for the place. But that's only my opinion. I'd rather live in a big city where I could meet other artists and paint people. I'd paint their fleshy outsides and the blue green veins pulsating through the skin. With ochres and white and cadmium red, I'd paint them inside out.

"Is this okay?" I gestured toward the perfectly cleaned sink.

"That's fine," she said.

I took my drawing tablet from the top of the refrigerator. "I'm going down to see if Marianne has time to cut my hair," I said.

"Okay." She was placing spice jars back onto the top shelf. *Jeop-*

ardy! was just beginning on the TV. "Turn up the sound a little, will you?"

In the garage Derriere stood on his toes, his whole body reaching to flick the switch that turned on the floodlights in the backyard.

"Hi," he said, turning suddenly. He looked guilty.

"What are you doing?" I asked.

"Nothing, just trying to turn the lights on. I can't see my trucks hardly." He stood stiffly, his back rigid against the garage wall. "Where are you going?" he asked.

"Down to get my hair cut."

"Marianne's kissing a man. She's smooching," he said. He made a face.

"Were you spying on them?" I asked.

"No! I saw them from the sandpile. Really gross stuff."

"Don't turn the lights on then, and don't go out there. It's none of your business." As soon as I said this, it occurred to me that maybe the man was Uncle Willy. Maybe Uncle Willy had come home. I reached at my throat to touch the silver armadillo that I still wore. Let it be true, Lord. I had to know.

"I want to play with my trucks," Derriere whined.

"Is it Willy? Is the man Uncle Willy?" I asked him.

He looked puzzled. "Didn't he wear a uniform?" he asked.

Exasperated, I grabbed his arm and led him out of the garage and through the chain-link gate that led to the backyard.

"Are we going to spy on them?" Derriere asked.

"Of course not," I said. "I just want to see if it's Willy."

"See," he said, when we had reached the sandpile. He pointed to Marianne's well-lighted basement living room. "We're spying, aren't we?"

"Not exactly," I whispered. Marianne and this guy—I could tell immediately he wasn't Willy—were standing in the middle of the living room in the tightest clutch I'd ever seen. They were clinging and squirming together like two worms in a fishing can, their faces mashed into each other. They had to be using their tongues.

"Yuck and double yuck," Derriere said.

"Shhh." The man was feeling around Marianne's back and waist and she was doing the same to him. I'm not an experienced kisser myself, although, as an artist, I am a careful observer. Once in a while I draw men and women embracing and kissing passionately, but I always throw those drawings away. It embarrasses me that I do that sometimes. It's kind of like kissing yourself in the mirror.

Marianne and her man, a tall man with dark hair not unlike Uncle Willy's, parted—for air, I guess. They laughed and then he kissed her on her neck and her cheeks and her eyes, and she moved her arms up about his neck and kissed him in front of his ear and on his chin.

"This is boring."

"Let's go back in the house," I said, not moving a millimeter.

Marianne and her boyfriend, whoever he was, were biting each other's lips. I thought I saw their tongues meet.

The first time I was kissed was when I was fourteen. Brian Chamberlain sat next to me in *The Electric Horseman,* starring Robert Redford and Jane Fonda. It was being shown in the gymnasium at school because the auditorium was being renovated. They always showed us some very romantic movie on Valentine's Day. Anyway, the first time Robert Redford—his name is Sonny Steele in the movie—kisses Jane Fonda, Brian Chamberlain lunges from his folding chair and kisses me. On the mouth. Probably somebody dared him to do it. I was too surprised to remember to close my eyes. I saw his two eyes become one. I saw individual hairs of his eyebrows and the pores of his skin. It wasn't much different than kissing the mirror. I mean, I didn't have any terrific out-of-body experience or anything. I didn't even have any terrific in-body experience. And why should I? I never even liked Brian Chamberlain. He was a jock and totally clueless about art.

When I told Fiona about it, she said I should have leaned into him a little. She said kissing required two people fully participating. And she said "art" had nothing to do with it. When Kenyon Braithwaite, whom I've known forever, kissed me on New Year's Eve while we were dancing in his basement, it embarrassed both of us. Fiona had something to say about that too. She said that (1) I was certainly easily embarrassed, and (2) as long as I insisted on perfection in everything, kissing partners included, I would certainly be disillusioned. Fiona, the gypsy prophetess.

I'll bet Willy was a good kisser.

Anyway, Marianne seemed to have a natural gift for kissing. I wondered if it was possible to bruise your lips from so much exercise. Certainly Marianne and her friend were candidates for severe bruising. Finally she pushed him away playfully, picked her handbag off the counter, swung the strap onto her shoulder, and opened her front door. We could hear their laughter and voices from the side of the house. Marianne switched the lights off, and the whole apartment grew black.

"Come on, let's go back this way," I said to Derriere. We entered the house through the garage.

The front doorbell was chiming.

Mother called to me from the bathroom. "Susan, are you there? Will you get the door, please?"

I shoved the car keys into my pocket and walked through the living room, Derriere following close behind. When I opened the front door, there stood Marianne and her friend, the mad kisser. He wasn't nearly as handsome as Willy. He had the same dark hair, but his teeth were slightly crooked and so was his nose, although he had nice eyes. His lips had that well-massaged look, but they weren't bruised. Marianne must have put on fresh lipstick before reaching our front door. Her face was red with blushing, and her eyes glittered like zircons.

"Is JoAnne decent?" she asked, pulling the screen door open.

"Mother!" I yelled. I stepped back into the living room and tried not to stare, although it was impossible not to.

Derriere just gawked. "Are you going to marry him?" he asked.

"The kid's psychic," the man said, smiling. He tousled Derriere's hair the way adults always do when they want to be friends with a child.

"I saw you kissing him in your apartment," Derriere said.

"Mother!" I yelled. "Marianne's here to see you."

"I'll be right there," she called back. The toilet flushed in the bathroom. You can hear it all over the house when the toilet flushes. It's pretty embarrassing.

"You saw us?" Marianne laughed. She put her arm around the man's waist. "Guess we should have pulled the blinds, huh?" She kissed his cheek. "This is Heber McIntyre. This is Derek and Susan, JoAnne's kids." We all nodded at each other.

"Susan saw you too. We were in the sandpile," Derriere said.

"Be quiet, Derriere," I said.

Mother walked in with a preoccupied, tense look on her face and then saw Heber McIntyre standing next to Marianne and shrieked, "Heber McIntyre—I can't believe it." She ran toward him and he toward her and they met in the middle of the room and hugged, and Heber McIntyre kissed my mother on the lips. It seemed odd to see a strange man kissing my mother that way. I mean, she's so very married, my mother is. They stood back from each other, Heber's hands still on my mother's waist and Mother holding on to his shoulders. "I am so glad to see you," Mother said.

"You are gorgeous as ever," Heber said. She had on this old sweat suit that belonged to my father. "You are as gorgeous as when I took you to the junior prom at Springville High."

Mother's head went back when she guffawed. "The worst date I ever had." She laughed.

"Me too," Heber said. "You wouldn't speak to me all night long."

"I had on my first strapless bra, and I was afraid it would fall down if I moved or talked." She covered her mouth when she giggled. They hugged each other again.

Marianne stood by, grinning and blushing. Derriere and I stood next to the upright piano and stared at this strange scene with our mother in it. I felt like we were still in the sandpile sneaking looks into the house.

"What are you doing here?" Mother asked him.

"I've come to steal your sister," Heber said.

Mother looked at Marianne for the first time since she had come into the room. "No!" she shrieked again. She hugged Marianne and then hugged Heber again. "This is terrific. Is it really true? Oh, it's wonderful," Mother gushed and then glanced at us. "Look at them. They think we're crazy."

I didn't disagree. There's this certain way adults are supposed to act, and this wasn't it. "Are you getting married?" I asked Marianne.

She nodded. "In May," she said.

"I have known Heber my whole life," Mother said to me. "He used to trip me up when I went to the blackboard in third grade."

"And I've had a crush on Heber my whole life," Marianne confessed. She held him around the waist. "I used to spy on him from afar."

Derriere looked up at me.

"Who did you like?" I asked Heber before Derriere could make another comment about spying.

"He liked Libby!" Mother and Marianne laughed together.

"That was in junior high," Heber said.

I was doing calculations in my head. When Heber was a senior, Marianne would have been in middle school and Libby would have been a freshman in college. Marianne started dating Willy when she was a senior. "What about Uncle Willy?" I didn't mean to say it, but it just sort of slipped out. How did he fit into all of this?

The three of them, a little stunned, I think, looked at each other, and then Marianne and Heber asked in unison, "Who's Willy?" and burst out laughing all over again.

It's about what I would have expected. Ever since Uncle Willy left ten years ago, no one in my family has wanted to talk about him. My hand automatically sought the silver armadillo at my throat. *I will not forget you, Willy,* I thought. *I will remember.*

Heber bent down on one knee in front of Derriere. "I'm going to be your uncle, champ. What do you think of that?"

Derriere looked down at his shoes and acted shy.

"You can come and visit me on my fishing boat," Heber continued. "You can help me catch salmon and crabs. Would you like that?"

Derriere nodded.

"You can visit us in Alaska." Heber stood up. "You too, Suzanne," he said.

"It's Sus5an—with a silent five," I said.

"Five?"

"Susan, for pity's sake," Mother said.

"I have a silent five in my name," I said.

Marianne laughed. "She's like Libby. Remember when she signed everyone's yearbook with lips drawn on end in place of the *b*'s in her name? She said her lips were silent."

Heber grinned. "I'll remember that silent five," he said to me, "if you'll come and visit us in Alaska."

"Sure," I said.

"I don't think I can stand it here without you," Mother said to Marianne.

"May I borrow the car for an hour?" I asked Mother. "Derriere and I want a Slurpee."

Heber smirked when he heard "Derriere." "She is like Libby, isn't she?" he said.

"Don't buy him any other sweets. He's going to lose all of his teeth," Mother warned.

"I won't," I lied. She had this big thing about the evils of sugar and the wonderfulness of wilted vegetables. She never cooked with sugar. Derriere was holding the screen door open for me. "See ya later," I said.

I wondered what would happen to Marianne's apartment. I wanted it for myself.

Later Derriere and I cruised up and down Main Street in the old Datsun, drinking strawberry Slurpees and eating Snickers bars. Driving through "Art City," I thought about Uncle Willy's replacement, Heber McIntyre. It hurt. I had hoped that Willy would return someday, but I realized that even if he did come back, Marianne wouldn't want him. Willy had been the one person who saw the world the same way I did, who understood the magic of seeing. That's what I thought. He didn't draw or paint like I did, but he "saw" things that other people didn't. I don't mean ghosts or weird stuff like that. I mean stuff like the way the sunlight comes in the kitchen window, the way the elm trees arch over our street, and the way the hollyhocks grow thick next to the garage. He appreciated the june bugs flitting about the yellow light of the porch. Willy saw it. He saw the magic of it. I'd probably never see him again. It hurt a lot.

❧ 3 ❧

I'm a portrait painter. I paint people the way I see them, which isn't always the way other people see them or even the way they see themselves. It's gotten me into trouble a few times. Like last year, when I entered a portrait of my father into the All High School Art Show—a statewide competition held at the Springville Museum. I painted him on the cover of a Wheaties box, dressed in his white grocer's coat, holding a fresh broccoli—you get it?— champion of grocers. It won a Master's Award, which is the highest you can go. Numero uno. The *Salt Lake Tribune* printed the painting in the Sunday-morning edition. But Mother, and Grandma too, weren't quite satisfied with it. They had wanted me to paint my father the way *they* would have painted him: sitting in his navy-blue Sunday suit in a leather wing chair holding a copy of *The Canterbury Tales* that my mother ordered from the Franklin Library in a moment of rare extravagance. Basically my whole family thinks art, and especially painting, is a frivolous pastime and that I am a frivolous person for pursuing it. They do approve of my sign painting for the market: Eggs, 79¢ a Dozen, and so on.

Anyway, the Wheaties portrait was last year. This year I managed to be even more offensive. It must be a gift. But I'm getting ahead of myself.

I got the idea for a kind of ancestral group portrait at Marianne's engagement dinner, which was held in one end of our living room on our dining room table with the extra leaf in it. Even then we could barely squeeze ten people around it. Heber's parents came, as well as Grandpa and Grandma Smith. It was Mrs. McIntyre's fault that I thought of it at all.

Marianne and Heber were rehashing their first date over dessert —cherry cobbler made with Mother's own canned cherries and French vanilla ice cream on top.

"His fly was open all night long!" Marianne laughed. Her hair was very blond and frizzed. She looked like Botticelli's Venus rising out of the shell.

"It was not," Heber said. He sat next to Mother, who sat at one head of the table. Mr. McIntyre, Heber's father, sat on the other side of her.

"It probably was," said Mrs. McIntyre. She was seated next to my dad. "You've always been very absentminded."

"Well, that's nothing," Heber said. "Marianne came to the door with a cold sore the size of a hamster on her top lip." He gestured with a rounded fist pointing at his face. "A humongous hamster— right here." He held the fist on his upper lip.

"Lip herpes," Derriere said.

We all laughed. I held a napkin to my lips to keep from spitting out the water I had in my mouth. Then we all sighed a collective sigh, and several people said, "That was a good one," and there was another sigh, and Grandma Smith broke in with, "It's too bad that Gaylen and Lucille can't be with us today." She looked over at Marianne. "They'd be so pleased."

It was like throwing black ash into our faces. Everyone had to get solemn immediately, because Gaylen and Lucille Schroeder, my mother's parents, had been dead for over thirteen years, while the rest of us were still very much alive, and having a good time to boot.

"That'd be nice, wouldn't it?" Marianne said politely.

And then Mrs. McIntyre said with a serious tone, "Perhaps they *are* here."

There was a pause while we all looked down at the food on our plates and considered the possible presence of the deceased Grandpa and Grandma Schroeder.

"I believe our loved ones who have passed away are still interested in the important events of our lives," Mrs. McIntyre continued. She looked significantly at Marianne and Heber.

"I do too," said Mother with a smile.

I was raised on religion, and I guess I believe in a life hereafter, but hearing Mrs. McIntyre talking about it over cherry cobbler, her voice kind of low and spooky like some female version of Vincent Price, made it all seem a bit hokey, even if it was a Sunday afternoon. So I let my mind wander a little.

I thought about Grandpa and Grandma Schroeder. I remembered Grandpa reading the funny papers to me aloud and Grandma letting me frost cookies in her kitchen. I knew them better from their snapshots: Grandpa, tall, bald, and very tan from playing golf all the time; and Grandma, her gray hair cropped short, seemed always to be laughing into the camera. I don't think she was anything like Grandma Smith, who wouldn't know a good joke if Bill Cosby himself told it to her. I imagined them sitting with us now at the dining room table: Grandma Schroeder laughing at Heber and Marianne's exaggerated stories of their romance, the many bracelets she always wore in each snapshot I'd ever seen of her tinkling lightly when she reached over to touch Grandpa's arm.

That's when I got the idea to do a family portrait—maybe like Da Vinci's *Last Supper,* only the figures seated around the table would be my parents and their parents and the aunts and uncles and Derriere and me. I liked the idea. I could work from photographs of Grandpa and Grandma Schroeder.

"I can't believe it's been thirteen years since the accident." Grandma Smith's voice interrupted my thoughts. She and

Grandma Schroeder had worked in the Relief Society together. Grandpa and Grandma Schroeder had been killed in a car crash in Provo Canyon when a truck, one of those eighteen-wheeler jobs, jackknifed in front of them on the icy road.

I thought about their being buried for thirteen years and wondered what they looked like *now.* Were their fingernails still growing, thirteen years later, in the Provo Cemetery?

It reminded me of the ancient cliff dwellers—the Anasazi. I called them the mummies. Daddy and I saw them in a tiny museum in southern Utah while Mother changed Derriere's diaper in the station wagon. They lay under glass in fetal positions, dead for hundreds of years. Some of their flesh remained, dried and dark, drawn tightly over the skull, the eye sockets hollow, the lips completely gone, exposing stained teeth. I wouldn't say they were smiling. They looked fragile under the glass and cold, their bodies folded gently. I stood longest in front of a mother with a baby in her arms, expecting to learn something from just staring at them. The shredded burlap wrappings were matted into the skin.

What is the difference between being dead thirteen years and being dead seven hundred years? And can you paint it? Can I?

The trouble with saying that my ancestral portrait would be like Leonardo's *Last Supper,* only with my family seated around the table instead of Christ and the apostles, is that then it isn't my painting at all. It's Leonardo's. It's *his* composition. Mr. Tuttle, my art teacher, is always telling us that we must find our own way of viewing the world.

"Try to find a new way of seeing." He says it over and over again. He's always talking about Picasso finding a new way to see. "Pablo was original." He calls Picasso by his first name like they were cousins or something.

When he gets intense, Mr. Tuttle wipes his bald head with the palm of his hand. He wipes the sweat off. It glistens on the top of his head, and he wipes it off. The trouble is, then he comes around and touches your arm with his sweaty hand. That bothers me. Still, I try to listen to what he says. I thought of it all through-out Marianne's engagement dinner.

I thought of Willy too. Where did he belong in the family portrait? Mother would say that he didn't belong in our family at all. But I could not expunge Willy like he never existed, never swung me in the August heat by my wrists and ankles, never kissed me good-bye on the cheek, never sent me a perfect silver armadillo necklace. I just couldn't let go of Willy. That's why he had to be included in the portrait.

Fiona called while Mr. and Mrs. McIntyre were leaving. I sat on the kitchen floor with the phone, because the chairs had all been put around the dining room table for extra seating.

"Listen up, Fiver," Fiona's voice shouted above the Pink Floyd singing in the background. "I'm filling out this housing application for the university, and I have to put down who I want for a roommate. Have you decided whether you're going to live on campus next fall with me, or are you going to live at home with your mommy and your daddy?"

"Very funny," I said. "I won't know until I find out if I got a scholarship. They should notify me any day now," I said.

Fiona groaned. "You've been saying that for weeks," she said. "If I put your name down, they'll wonder who Susan, silent five, Smith is if you don't also apply—"

"I know, but—"

"So I was thinking . . ." Fiona was getting ready to organize me. "Why don't you go ahead and apply now, and then if it turns out that you don't get the scholarship, you can just turn down the housing, and I'll have to room with an alien."

Mother looked into the kitchen and said, "Susan, they're leaving. Come and say good-bye."

I nodded at her. "Okay," I said to Fiona. "I'll apply."

"Great. That was easy."

Marianne stuck her head into the doorway and blew me a kiss and waved.

I scrambled to my feet and straightened my dress. "My aunt's leaving. I've got to go say good-bye," I told Fiona.

"Don't forget."

"I won't. 'Bye."

Grandpa and Grandma Smith stayed even after the rest had gone home. Dad and Grandpa read the Sunday papers on the living room sofa while Grandma and Mother put the leftovers into the refrigerator. Derriere was whining because he had to clear the dining room table.

I sat on the piano bench and sketched Grandpa's face. Already the painting that I would do was forming, however vaguely, in my head. It would be better than the painting of Dad on the Wheaties box. It would be a more ambitious painting.

"Take away my double chins, will you?" Grandpa said, not looking up from his newspaper.

"Then it wouldn't be you," I said.

"There was a time when I didn't have double chins," he said.

"I don't remember it."

"It wasn't that long ago. How old are you?"

"Seventeen."

"It wasn't that long ago," he repeated.

"Yes it was," Dad said. He folded his paper and laid it in his lap. "You had double chins when I got married, and that's been almost twenty years now."

"Did not," Grandpa muttered, trying to press the chins into his neck.

"Did too."

"You have double chins too," I said to Dad. "It must be hereditary."

"Ha!" Grandpa looked over his paper.

"I don't have double chins," Dad said.

"Yes, you do," I said.

"Ha, ha, ha," Grandpa mocked. He walked across the room and sat down on the piano bench with me. "When I die," he said to me, "I'm going to give you all of my money. Every last penny."

"A whole dollar fifty. You'll be rich, Susan." Daddy stretched out on the sofa and adjusted the pillows under his head.

"You are some artist." Grandpa watched me sketch. "She's made us both look almost respectable," he said to my father.

"I don't flatter people," I said. "If you look respectable, then you are respectable."

"Oh, excuse me," Grandpa said.

"Rightly so," said my dad.

Mother walked into the room. "Susan, I want you to come in and help Grandma and me do the dishes, please," she said. She wore an apron that had *Sunday Apron* lettered on the front of it. Grandma made it for her last year for Mother's Day.

"Okay, just a minute," I said. "I'm almost done with this drawing."

"The drawing can wait. Now, please."

"The drawing always has to wait," I said. "The dishes never wait. Drawing is my work," I said. "Painting is my work. Do you want me to ruin my hands?"

"We'll rinse, and you stack. That way your hands will be preserved," she said.

Grandpa gently shoved me off the piano bench. "Go and help your mother," he whispered. "I'll model for you when you get back."

"With your clothes off?" I asked.

"If you can stand it, so can I."

In the kitchen the dishes were heaped to the ceiling with gobs of zucchini and onion casserole cemented to them. Mother's face reflected the sunlight from the window over the sink. I would paint the crease in her forehead. I would paint the tension. I would paint Grandma's tension too. They were both afraid, I realized. I didn't want to grow up and be afraid.

It isn't enough to paint an accurate portrait. Anyone can learn to do it with practice. A good portrait must also be a good painting. Mr. Tuttle said so. It must be a fine painting.

Grandma let out a little shriek as she dropped a china plate. It fractured into pieces on the tile floor. "It slipped right through my fingers. I'll buy you another one," she said to my mother.

"Don't be silly," Mother said.

"Let me get it," I said. I bent over the pieces of porcelain. They had formed a kind of square on the floor and looked like parts of a jigsaw puzzle laid out on an old card table ready for someone to fit them together. Like puzzle pieces, the broken china had uniform triangular shapes as if they would fit into each other easily. I began to pick them up and place them in a grocery bag from Russell's Market. I know it sounds dumb, but there was a kind of joy and magic for me in having the plate shatter into a square instead of the pieces spinning off into all the corners of the room—as if it had formed its own painting on an invisible canvas. Except for one piece. It lay under the edge of the cupboard.

"Grandma, move your foot a little. There's one more piece under here." I picked it up. It was round. It didn't look like it fit with the rest of the plate, yet it clearly was a part of it. I threw it in the sack with the rest of the pieces and tossed the whole bag into the garbage can in the garage.

"Do you think Libby will come out for Marianne's wedding?" Grandma was asking Mother.

"I hope so. It will be the last opportunity for us to be together for a while, with Marianne going to Alaska." She sighed. "We'll be all over the place: Utah, Massachusetts, Alaska . . ." Her voice trailed off.

"You're going to miss Marianne, aren't you? Russell's at the store all the time. It's been kind of nice for you and Marianne to have each other."

"It has," Mother said.

"I wish I had a pot of money to give you," Grandma said, turning on the faucet for more hot water. "Russell could get some more help, and the two of you could go on a nice trip together. Just a small potful of money. A little skip."

Mother laughed. "We could use a small potful of money," she said.

"I guess you're going to rent the apartment?"

"We'll have to."

"Oh, please let me have the apartment," I said. "I could use it for a studio. Please, Mom, please. I need the room. I barely have room for my easel and stuff." I held on to her arm. My room was a small, converted back porch.

Mother let the plug out of the sink and shook her hands loose of soapsuds. "We need the income."

"I can hardly move in my room," I said.

"I know it's tiny—"

"Pshaw," Grandma interrupted. "I had a room smaller than yours when I was a girl, and I had to share it with my sister. I have never had a room of my own in my entire life."

"Then you shouldn't have gotten married," I said.

"Susan!" Mother turned and stared at me in disbelief.

"Sorry," I said to Grandma. Now she'd rail on about how she had to walk all over Utah County as a girl with the soles of her shoes all worn out. I could hear the imaginary violin strings warming up for her tragic childhood stories.

"You just don't appreciate what you have, miss. Your room may be small, but it's yours. And you have good shoes on your feet." The dish towel she'd been using fluttered with the gesturing of her hand. "I used to have to walk to Spanish Fork from Springville, and my shoes were practically gone. I would just cry sometimes, my feet hurt so much."

"I know," I said. "In the snow."

"Yes. Sometimes in the snow." She nodded her head up and down for emphasis. "It got very cold in *those* days."

Mother smiled in spite of herself. "I would give you the apartment if I could, but I just can't. We simply cannot give up that income. I'm sorry," she said.

"Maybe we'll win one of those magazine sweepstakes," I said. "Ed McMahon himself will hand us the ten million dollars on TV."

Mother patted my bangs back from my forehead. "I think you have a better chance of contracting brain cancer," she said.

"Those contests are all fixed anyway," Grandma said.

"I'll just have to become a famous painter," I said.

"Or a teacher," Mother and Grandma said at the same time.

In my room I drew a perfect square with a ruler and then sketched the pieces of broken plate inside the square. I thought again about the remains of the cliff dwellers lying in fetal positions under glass and of my mother's parents lying separately in shiny, metallic boxes lined with satin. Did they look as dead as the cliff dwellers? I thought about Mr. Tuttle's bald head bobbing intensely at me: "A portrait must also be a good painting."

And then I got the idea for my painting. It came from inside of me. I knew exactly what it would look like: I would paint jigsaw pieces lying on the surface of an old card table. In each of the jigsaw pieces, I would paint a face: mine, my parents', both sets of grandparents', Libby's and Marianne's and Heber's too, since he would now be part of the family. Some of the pieces would be connected, like Mother's and Daddy's with mine and Derriere's. Those four pieces would be connected. And I would connect Heber's with Marianne's piece. Grandma Smith would be connected to Grandpa Smith. Grandma Schroeder would be connected to Grandpa Schroeder. Libby's piece would be disconnected, off by itself, but even though the pieces were not all connected, they would be obvious parts of the same puzzle, all the pieces having the same rounded configuration.

Except for one piece. It would be a perfect triangle off to one side of the table's surface and would never fit with the other pieces. And it would have Uncle Willy's face painted on it.

⤜ 4 ⤛

Once I begin a painting, I keep my bedroom door locked. Daddy
put this double-duty dead bolt on my door years ago when Mother
was afraid Derriere would get into my room and guzzle a glass of
paint thinner. Unfortunately he never did this. Now I keep it
locked, because I don't want to hear questions like, "Why are you
painting our faces as puzzle pieces?" or "Why are you putting that
S.O.B. Willy Gerard into a family portrait?" And I especially don't
want to hear, "Why are Grandma and Grandpa Schroeder's faces
distorted on one side?"

"They are like the mummies now," I would say. And that
wouldn't be good enough.

I worked on the painting every spare minute I had that spring,
and when it was finished, I knew it was good. I knew it was very
good. No one in my family had seen it. I packed it up and had
Fiona pick me up in her truck and drive me to the high school so I
could show Mr. Tuttle. I was sure the portrait wouldn't fit into our
cramped old Datsun. Fiona dropped me off and said she'd meet
me out in front of the school in twenty minutes; she had to run to
the post office for her mother.

Mr. Tuttle was waiting for me. "Ah, there you are," he said,
looking up from his desk. His fingers were stained with charcoal

and colored chalk. "Let's have a look." He got up and walked around his desk and began to untie the rope that held the padding in place. He was wearing his trout tie—a large scaly fish he had painted onto vinyl, the trout's head at the bottom of the tie. He wore it all the time.

I waited for him to say something; I couldn't stand the silence. "It's a portrait of my whole family," I couldn't help saying. "It's everybody. Even my Uncle Willy, who's been gone for ten years. Nobody knows where he is. He deserted the air force and my aunt on the same day. The FBI comes around and asks about him every once in a while." I didn't know why I was telling him my whole family history, but I couldn't shut up. I pointed to the sharp triangular shape at the top of the painting. "He was really nice," I added.

He wiped his bald head with the palm of his hand. "Incredible," he said. "Who—what's this here?" He pointed to the hollow-eyed skull of the cave-dweller woman with the partially decayed baby in her arms. Her puzzle piece was connected to Grandpa and Grandma Schroeder's, who had half of their faces eaten away— looking like the cave dwellers. The other half of their faces looked like their photographs—smiling. "It's a mummified Anasazi woman and her baby. I saw them in a museum once. I've never been able to get them out of my mind," I said. "These are my grandparents, who have been dead for thirteen years."

He stared at them. "Jeez!" He blew it out with his breath like it was involuntary. His hand seemed glued to the back of his bald pate. "What did your parents say when they saw it?" He kept his eyes on the painting.

"They haven't seen it. They'll see it when the exhibition opens. They don't know anything about painting anyway. My mother wants me to paint flowers."

He nodded his head. "I can imagine," he muttered.

"What do you think?" I finally asked.

His hand came off his head and held on to the trout tie, flipping the end with the trout head nervously back and forth. "Well," he said, "this is the best student painting I've ever seen."

"Really?"

"It's not just the technique. It's the whole concept. It's simply— it's, well, if I painted this good, I wouldn't be teaching high school."

"Really?"

"Absolutely."

"You think it's good?"

"I think it's art."

"Really?"

"Don't you know?" he asked.

"I thought it was good. I didn't know if it was good enough."

"It's sensational. I predict you'll take the whole show."

"Really?"

He looked straight at me. "What's this *really* bit? I wouldn't say it if I didn't think so. This is one fine painting."

I squealed. "Yippee Skippy!"

"Yippee Skippy?" He laughed and sat down on his desk.

"Pablo always said that when he finished a painting."

"He did, huh." He laughed. He sat with his arms folded in front of him. "May I offer a suggestion?"

"You're the teacher," I said.

"I think you should show it to your family before the opening night of the exhibition. It's going to shock them. Give them time to get used to it."

Fiona had essentially said the same thing the first time she had seen it: "You're not going to show it to them before the exhibition? They'll freak out right there in front of everybody. They'll freak. Wait and see."

"Oh, they won't either," I had said. But I wasn't at all sure.

To Mr. Tuttle I said, "They won't want me to show it. My mother will forbid it." Actually I didn't know this, but it sounded dramatic. I didn't like him siding with my parents. "They won't understand," I said. "They're real philistines when it comes to art."

"They're your family." He was looking at the ends of his black, square-tipped cowboy boots.

"No," I said more emphatically. "I don't want them interfering." My voice rose to a slightly hysterical pitch.

He motioned for me to stop with his hands. "Okay, okay. It was only a suggestion."

"As a matter of fact I was wondering if you'd keep it in your office until the show. I really don't want them to see it. I don't want to risk it at all."

"Sure." He stood up.

"Thanks a lot," I said. "You really think it's good, huh?"

"I think you're a star," he said.

I spotted the black Mazda truck in the visitors' parking lot in front of the high school. Fiona's naked feet dangled out of the open window on the driver's side, the ankles twisting about irregularly to the beat of the music blaring from the radio—Def Leppard. She jerked herself upright when I opened the door. "What'd you do with the painting?" she asked, turning the radio down.

"He's going to keep it for me until the show."

She started up the engine. "Why?" She shifted the truck into reverse.

"So my parents can't see it."

"They still haven't seen it?" The truck lunged out of the parking lot.

"Nope."

"I thought you weren't going to do that anymore after last year." She was referring to the Wheaties portrait of my father.

"Changed my mind."

"My mother would kill me if I painted that portrait of our family. She'd have me drawn and quartered just for painting all that death, and we don't even have an Uncle Willy in our family."

Fiona knew of my devotion to the missing Willy. She braked too quickly for a light and jolted us forward. "Your mother and Marianne are going to croak," she said.

"Get real," I said, and turned up the radio so loud that we couldn't talk anymore. But Mr. Tuttle's and especially Fiona's reaction did worry me a little bit. Maybe I shouldn't have made Grandpa and Grandma Schroeder and the Anasazi woman the focal point of the painting. Maybe I shouldn't have put Uncle Willy in there. They would want to know why I did it.

And I didn't have the answers. Even old Pablo P. was contemptuous of the way everybody and his dog wanted to understand art. He said why not try to understand the songs of birds? He said artists work of necessity. My painting came from inside of me. It came from my family, from the cave dwellers, from a broken plate after Sunday dinner. It came from loving and missing Willy Gerard, who was once my uncle. I still wore the armadillo necklace around my neck. The thin, delicate chain had never been broken. How could I explain that to someone like my mother, who was blind to visual nuance? I asked her once what she thought was so beautiful about Springville, Utah. She was planting zucchini starts in the vegetable garden out back.

"The mountains," she said, without looking up.

A standard answer. Ask anyone in Utah what they think is beautiful and they say mountains. I don't disagree, but they're so obvious—jutting out all over the place as they do. They're the Rocky Mountains, for pity's sake.

"Well, what time of day do you like the mountains best?" I asked my mother.

"Anytime of day," she said. "I like them every time I look up at them."

"I know, but the light changes. In what light do you like them best?"

"I like them in any light. Haven't you got something to do besides standing out here and asking me funny questions?"

Willy would have answered differently: "Well, girl," he'd say, "I like them best in black light."

"What's black light?" I'd ask.

"It's those few minutes just before the sun sets completely and the mountains are a deep, deep purple with patches of light—that's the scrub oak—it's a lighter color. And if you stand very still and watch the mountains in the black light, they look as if they're breathing. Mountains move. They shimmer, girl. They shimmer in the black light."

I'm almost positive that's what Willy would say about the light on the mountains. He had what I would call an artistic vision. It's what I missed in the people around me. I couldn't change my painting for them just because they didn't understand.

No, the painting was just right.

I became a housepainter too. Mother wanted our dilapidated house to look perfect for the first week in May when Aunt Libby would come from Boston for Marianne's wedding. It was the same week that the All High School Art Show would begin at the Springville Museum with my family portrait displayed for everyone to see. I helped Mother paint the living room and kitchen walls. I helped her steam-clean the carpets, which were bare as a bug's behind. We cleaned crannies and moldings and the underbellies of cabinets. We reorganized the kitchen cabinets a dozen times. We did windows. We cleaned until the house smelled like the inside of a Lysol container. We kept up our strength with wilted-vegetable casseroles.

Fiona and I both received letters from the university confirming our housing with each other. I had received a full scholarship, so I could afford to live on campus if I maintained some kind of part-time job. Fiona was ecstatic. "Everything is going according to plan," she told me. "It's perfect." She was the oldest of eight brothers and sisters, so going off to college to live with me seemed like a vacation to her. I tried to shove the feeling down, but going to the university so close by seemed oppressively conventional and artless.

It was as if I lived inside a Bruegel painting, among peasants, domestic, hardworking, plain, and grotesque. They dreamed their peasant dreams. They were not my dreams. I dreamed of being lifted up by a dozen pink and ivory babies, trailing white rose petals that wafted and fluttered to the ground below. The babies, so fat and lovely, floated me up, up, parting the clouds—floating me up past the mountains, over the mountains, and away from the mountains.

Like royalty, Aunt Libby arrived with a flourish of trumpets. She brought packages wrapped in shiny paper from Jordan Marsh and Filene's.

"It's just like Christmas when you come," I exclaimed. The living room floor was littered with wrappings and ribbons.

"Old-maid aunts must come bearing gifts or they're not welcome," Libby said. She helped Derriere get his arms through the Boston Red Sox sweatshirt she had brought him.

"I am sure," drawled Mother. She was already stuffing debris into a trash bag. "I've never seen anyone who looks less like an old maid. How do you stay so thin? You look more like Susan's sister than mine."

It was true. She looked young and dressed young. I would have killed to have a pair of leather boots like hers. Her hair hung loose down her back.

"You must watch what you eat, huh?" Mother asked.

"She's a carrot freak," I said.

"Actually, no. I only eat things like Snickers bars and drink Mountain Dew. I've given up meat and vegetables and grains and polyunsaturates."

"Awright!" Derriere and I said in chorus.

"Thanks a lot," Mother nudged her playfully with the trash bag. "Try and set an example, will you?"

"Aunts don't have to set examples. Their duty is to bring gifts and act eccentric."

"Oh, brother," Mother puffed.

"What's 'sentric'?" Derriere asked.

"It means," Dad said, "that your Aunt Libby has a bit of the cuckoo on her breath."

"I reek of cuckoo." Libby laughed.

"You're strange," Derriere said, grinning at her.

"I hope so," Libby said.

The front door bell rang, and without waiting for someone to answer it, Marianne pushed it open and stepped inside, Heber McIntyre following behind.

"It's baby!" Libby shrieked. She lifted herself off the floor and collapsed into Marianne's arms.

While they were hugging and laughing, I looked old Heber over, and sure enough, he had well-massaged lips again. He must have lost all feeling in them by now.

"I'm so sorry I couldn't meet you, but Heber drove down from Seattle, and I was expecting him any minute, give or take an hour," Marianne said in a breathless rush.

"I understand perfectly." Libby laughed. She peeked around Marianne's shoulder. "Hello, Heebie," she said.

"Hello, Libby Lou," Heber said. Libby moved around Marianne and grabbed Heber around the neck. "You still wuv me?" she asked him.

"Always, dearest," he said in a sappy tone. They kissed on the lips. I didn't know about Libby, but Heber had had plenty of practice.

"How come you didn't blush like that when I kissed you?" Mother asked.

Dad exploded with laughter at the goofy look on Heber's face.

Marianne and Mother sang in unison, "Heebie loves Libby. Heebie loves Libby!" until Heber's head might as well have been a tomato—he was that red.

"I thought Heber was marrying *Marianne,*" Derriere shouted over the silliness.

Mother put her hand over her mouth and snickered helplessly. "He is. He is. Libby is an old friend of Heber's. We're all old friends of Heber's," she said. They broke out in giggles again.

❧ 5 ❧

The whole family, including Grandma and Grandpa, went to the All High School Art Show at the Springville Museum in Heber's van. I had asked Fiona if she wanted to come too, but she said she had already arranged to go with Kenyon Braithwaite and Natalie White. "It's safer than being with your family at the unveiling, so to speak," she had said. I called her chicken, and she clucked hysterically for me. Derriere was dropped off at Spencer Wheelwright's house because, as he put it, "I don't want to go to no stupid art show." I already knew I had won a prize, because I had received a letter during the week telling me so.

"I'll bet you've won another Master's Award," Daddy said. He and Mother were sitting in the middle seat with Grandma and Grandpa. I sat in the very back with Libby.

"I hope so," I said. To tell the truth, I'd be hopping mad if I won anything less than the Master's Award. I knew the painting was the best I'd ever done. You just know those things. But I was nervous about my family seeing it, and my hands were all sweaty, even though I kept rubbing them on my skirt.

"And we're all in it?" Libby asked.

"It's a family portrait. You're all in it. Even Heber, since he'll be a member of the family on Monday."

Heber and Marianne exchanged a smile in the front seat.

"Well, I'm eager to see it," Daddy said.

Mother must not have been so sure, because she was silent.

Heber parked the van directly across the street from the museum, which had lots of people wandering in and out of the open front doors. I was pretty nervous. They weren't going to like it. It wouldn't just be Mother; none of them would like it.

We walked en masse up the brick walk that fronted the museum, past Dennis Smith's statue of the little girls holding their baby brother. The building glittered with light. In the front hall a woman handed us a program and pointed to the room in front of us, where a buffet table was set up and an all-saxophone band played. I turned to my left to look into what I always considered to be the main gallery, and there was my painting in the center of the back wall behind the chairs that were set up for the awards presentation. It was by far the largest painting in the room, and it was, I thought, in the best position.

I swallowed hard. "It's on the back wall," I said, nodding toward it. "The big one." The whole family shifted left.

"Looks like you get center stage," Libby said to me.

"It doesn't look like a family portrait from here." Grandma sniffed.

Mother squinted down the long hall, her face pinched and tight.

I looked distractedly for Fiona but didn't see her among the clusters of people gathered in front of the paintings around the room.

We made our way around the chairs. A woman and a young boy were standing in front of my painting, and so we sort of spread ourselves around and in back of them.

"There are dead people in there," the boy said to his mother. "How come they're dead?" He pointed at the Anasazi woman and her baby. "They're dead, aren't they?"

"Yes, shhh," the mother whispered to him.

"What's the matter with these people? Are they half-dead? Are they sick or something?" His finger touched Grandma Schroeder's partially decayed face.

I heard Mother gasp, although I couldn't see her. She stood behind me.

"Don't touch the painting, Jason," the woman said. "I think they're dead too. See how the puzzle pieces are connected with the dead woman?" She took a deep breath. "Move to the side, Jason, and let these people see too." She pulled on his arm.

"Oh, my laws, girl, what could you be thinking?" Grandma held her hand across her lips. No one said anything. We stood as if paralyzed, held together with a familial thread. We stood in a terrible silence that seemed to last forever.

"Have you seen this one?" a girl about my age asked her friend. "I wish I'd painted this one myself. I mean, look at all those smiley faces gazing out of the puzzle pieces and then all of this death in the center here. It's spooky."

"It's grotesque," the other girl said. "It's neat too. It's like the only way all the puzzle pieces can be joined together is if they die. You know what I mean? These people out here," she gestured with her hand, "when they die, they'll move into the middle and join with these center pieces. Isn't that what it feels like?"

"I told you it was spooky," the other girl said. They walked around us.

I liked her idea of the other pieces coming together in death. I hadn't thought of it myself, but I liked it a lot.

Still, no one in my family spoke, and I wasn't sure that they ever would. Heber cleared his throat a couple of times.

Finally Libby, who wiped moisture away from one eye, said, "It's an extraordinary and painful work, Susan." Her voice was unusually husky. "I had no idea you were so gifted."

"It may be a good painting," Grandma said quickly, "but I sure don't want you painting me after I'm dead and gone and can't defend myself. That's all I can say. Let's sit down," she said to Grandpa, and walked away.

I didn't have to turn my head to know that Mother was also walking away. Daddy went after her.

Libby slipped her arm through mine and kept it there.

Heber, his arm around Marianne, said, "I'm glad she's got you joined with the right puzzle piece—me." He smiled at me. I was so grateful for that smile.

"She's got us right where we belong," Marianne said. They squeezed each other's middles. "I think Willy would be flattered that you still want him in the family," Marianne said, turning to me. "I'm sure it's the only real family he ever had—before or since. It's painful—like Libby said—but it's wonderful too." She leaned over and kissed my cheek.

"Thank you," I said.

She and Heber moved on to look at other paintings, murmuring quietly to each other.

"I like it very much," Libby said again. We were the only two left standing in front of my painting, our arms still locked together.

I turned to look over my shoulder at Mother, her back slumped into a folding chair. Daddy had his arm around her, whispering to her. "She's never going to speak to me again," I said, and realized that my chin was quivering dangerously.

Libby turned her head to glance at Mother and turned back. "It's hard to be the mother of an artist like you're turning out to be," she said. "You've done something painful here—something shocking—yes, shocking." She repeated it, because I must have looked surprised. "You didn't really expect her to like it, did you? Be honest."

"No."

"JoAnne isn't going anywhere. She's just catching her breath. You'll see."

"I—I—" We stepped back to allow a group of people to pass through.

"Yes?"

"I can't paint differently," I said. "I can't ignore what's in me."

Libby sighed heavily. "I wonder where old Willy is," she mused. She stared at his picture. "I thought I saw him in Harvard Square —twice actually—but I was too far away to tell for sure, and by the time I was closer, he had disappeared."

"You saw Willy?"

"I *thought* I saw him. I may have been wrong."

"Mother says he's in hell."

Libby laughed. "I doubt it," she said. "He's too wily for hell."

"He was my favorite uncle."

"He was your *only* uncle," Libby said.

"He used to grab me by my ankles and hands and swing me around the backyard. It was so much fun. And he liked the pictures I drew, and he wasn't like other adults, he—"

"He wasn't an adult at all," Libby interrupted. "But he was charming."

"Yes, he was charming," I said.

"Don't confuse him with Prince Charming, though," she said. "He wasn't Prince Charming, Susan."

"Uncle Charming?"

She smiled. "Yeah, I guess he could have been Uncle Charming."

"He sure was handsome as Zeus," I said.

Libby looked at me. "Let's walk through the other rooms and then sit down," she suggested.

A lot of the paintings were copied straight out of *National Geographic* magazine. You know the kind of stuff I mean—Arabs sitting in front of a tent. I mean, where in Utah are you going to find a bunch of Arabs sitting in front of a tent? There was one painting of a Bolivian mother and her child. She was wearing one of those round felt hats that Bolivian women wear—straight out of *National Geographic.* I think I remember seeing that exact picture. Why didn't the artist paint her own mother and sister? It would have been so much more interesting and honest. Of course if I had

painted some Bolivian family instead of my own, I wouldn't have
been as estranged from my mother as I felt right then.

Kenyon was at the water fountain in the hall. "Where's Fiona?"
I asked him.

He nodded down the hall. "In the john. Nat's saving us a seat. I
really liked your painting," he said. "You're just a little spooky,
Sue."

"So I'm finding out."

Libby nudged me. "We'd better locate our own seats." she said.

"See ya later," I told Kenyon.

Libby and I sat next to Marianne and Heber, who were seated
behind my parents and grandparents. Dad turned around and
squeezed my knee. Mother sat rigid in her seat, looking forward.

Finally the man, who had been torturing us with the sound
system by repeating "Testing, one—two—three" into it and
thumping it vigorously with his open palm, officially welcomed us.
He told us there were 440 pieces of art displayed out of 800
entries from all over the state. Blah, blah, blah, blah. There were
three Master's Awards with a cash prize of one hundred dollars
each. "May I have the envelopes, please." The audience snickered
at the obvious. "The first Master's Award goes to Susan Smith of
Springville High."

Daddy let out a whoop and a "brava" and clapped boisterously.

"Way to go, Susan." Heber leaned across Marianne and Libby.

In the back a section of kids stood up and cheered. I recognized
Fiona's wolf whistle even before I saw her. I couldn't help but grin.
I moved across the aisle, my aunts congratulating me as I went. To
my relief Mother clapped too, her tightly compressed lips in a half
smile.

Mr. Tuttle stepped out of the group of art teachers standing off
to the side and handed me a certificate and an envelope with a
check in it. "You deserve it," he said to me.

"Thanks for all your help," I said. We shook hands.

The emcee pointed out my painting to the audience. Collective heads turned to have a look at it. "The judges want to know how you pronounce that five in your name." He pulled me closer to the microphone.

"It's a silent five," I said. "It's just Susan Smith. The five is a visual statement." It sounded so stupid. I wished I'd never invented it.

The group of kids in the back shouted approval.

The rest of the audience tittered politely and clapped again as I walked back to my seat. Mother's face smiled at me tentatively. I smiled back.

The other Master's Awards were handed out. One was for a watercolor that was an obvious copy of a Calvin Klein ad. I tried not to think about it, but it irritated me anyway.

When it was over, Grandpa came around and kissed me. "What are you going to do with that hundred dollars?" he asked.

"Buy more paint," I said.

"Laws!" Grandma puffed. "You sure are an obsessed child."

"And aren't you glad?" Fiona interrupted and hugged me. "Congratulations!" she said.

Grandma stepped back into the row of seats to make way for my friends. Kenyon and Nat hugged me too. Jennifer made a half bow and said she was awed in my presence. Danny Ellison gave me a high five, and Wayne Ikhaml blew kisses and I blew them back. Their noisy silliness and laughter made me feel better.

"We're going to a drive-in in Wayne's Jeep; can you come?" Jennifer asked.

I looked at my family huddled in a group, obviously waiting for me. "I don't think so," I said. "They're having a little family gathering at home—"

"How'd your mother take it?" Fiona whispered, aware that Mother was close by.

"Okay—sort of," I whispered back.

"Sure you can't come? It's still a half hour before dark."

"I'd better not."

The group groaned in what seemed like practiced unity and then laughed at themselves. I was patted and congratulated again, and then they moved down the aisle, a mass of elbows and knees. I could hear their laughter and chatter even when they were outside in the hallway, and wished desperately that I could escape with them.

At the house Mother and Grandma fixed banana splits in the kitchen. The others sat in the living room. Dad moved nervously back and forth between the two rooms. "Do you need any help?" he asked Mother not once but three times.

I was sitting on a dining room chair with a partial view of the kitchen.

"No, I said I didn't." I could barely hear my mother's lowered, but clearly irritated voice. "Why do you keep asking? Just go in and sit down with the others." She stuck the opened bottle of hot fudge into the microwave to soften it.

"Look, I know you're mad," he said. He stood by the door now.

I glanced at the others in the living room to see if they could hear my parents fighting, but Libby and Heber sat together on the piano bench and went through high school all over again by looking at Mother's yearbooks and telling stories that happened some twenty-odd years before. Marianne stood behind the two of them, searching for outrageous hairdos. They were too engrossed and too noisy themselves to pay attention to what was going on in the kitchen. Grandpa sat on the sofa and watched them.

"I am not mad," my mother insisted, but she wouldn't look at him and only stared at the microwave-oven door.

"Well, it's none of my business, but I wouldn't blame you if you were mad," Grandma chirped. She scooped chocolate chip ice cream into the banana split dishes. "She just humiliated the whole family—that's what she did—and what she did to your parents! I tell you, I could just cry."

My ears burned when I realized she was discussing me, and I

leaned forward into the living room more, my head turned away from them, so that they wouldn't know I was listening.

The microwave-oven door shut with a louder bang than was necessary.

"Are you still upset about the painting? Is that what this is all about?" My dad had lowered his voice.

"No, I'm not upset," Mother said at the same time that Grandma said, "Of course she's upset."

"It's only a painting . . ." my dad said.

"Is it?" Mother's voice rose.

"You're just spoiling her," Grandma said.

"What do you want me to do? Chain her up and say, 'No, you can't ever paint again. It upsets your mother and your grandmother.'"

Mother's voice was exasperated. "Give me a break."

"She needs to learn responsibility." That's Grandma's favorite word. She tends to say it with capital letters.

"Give *me* a break," Daddy said, leaving the kitchen. He sat on the sofa next to Grandpa.

"That was called a butterfly," Marianne was still pointing at hairdos. "There." Her index finger touched the page. "Emily Smoot. I'll bet she could kill herself when she looks at it now."

"Hey, I dated her," Heber said.

"You dated everyone," Dad said from the sofa.

"You're just jealous because I had a hot date with JoAnne before you did," Heber said.

Mother, who now carried a large tray of banana splits, managed a half smile for Heber. "It was a two-word date: *hi* and *'bye.'*"

"JoAnne told me all about that date," Dad said. He lifted a banana split off the tray. He and Mother did not look at each other at all. "She said the hottest thing about it was that the Beatles sang 'Why Don't We Do It in the Road' on the car radio on the way home."

Without signaling one another, Libby, Heber, and Marianne began singing in their best simulated Beatle voices, "Why don't we do it in the road?" It was as if mentioning the Beatles had created a magic spell. They rose out of their seats and began dancing as well. Their bodies lurched, swayed, and twisted in rhythmic alliance. "Why don't we do it in the road?" Grandma, who was passing paper napkins to everyone, muttered, "I didn't like this music then and I don't like it now—why don't we do *what* in the road?"

The dancing adults, hearing Grandma's question, collapsed on each other in guffaws like a bunch of goofy drunks. Even Dad had to smile. Mother was setting the banana splits on the piano for Libby, Heber, and Marianne, and I couldn't see her face.

Grandma's lips only compressed tighter. "The world's gone clear crazy," she said to Grandpa, who stopped smiling when she said it. "Hurry and eat. I want to go home." She sat at the edge of the sofa, ready to spring up.

At Libby's request my father pulled out his old guitar and accompanied Heber, who sang the verses of "Hey Jude." He had a pleasantly mellow voice that filled the room. We listened, our heads tilted slightly. Libby mouthed the words while he sang. Mother sat at the far end of the room, near the front door, spooning ice cream into her mouth very slowly, a pained expression behind her eyes. We all sang the chorus except Grandma, who examined her hands and fingernails, which lay in her lap.

"Oh, how I loved—*love* the Beatles." Libby sighed when it was over.

Grandma stood up. "We've got to go," she said briskly. She took Grandpa's dish and her own, neither of which was completely eaten, and headed for the kitchen. "We'll leave through the garage. Come on, Floyd," she called to Grandpa, but he stopped by my chair and whispered to me: "This is a supporting grant for the Master's Award." He slipped a couple of bills into my hands, patted my shoulder, and followed Grandma into the kitchen. It was a hundred dollars.

"We've got to go too," Marianne said. She and Heber moved

toward the door and thanked my mother. "Congrats again, Sue," Heber called.

"Love you," Marianne called to me from across the room, and blew me a kiss.

"I'll do the dishes," Libby offered, collecting the empty dishes.

I went to my room and lay on my bed, staring at the pink bridesmaid's dress for Marianne's wedding hanging on the closet door. A slight summer breeze stirred the curtains gently in the open window. My painting had been the best in the show. I could see it. Mr. Tuttle could see it. A lot of people could see it, but I had hurt my family, especially my mother and my grandmother, by painting it. Should I not have painted it? Was there something wrong with me in thinking up such a painting? But how could I not paint it?

There's a photograph of Picasso sitting in his studio, a large whitewashed room with richly carved moldings on the walls and ceilings. His canvases are leaning against the walls, and he himself straddles a wooden chair in the center of the room, his arms crossed casually against the back of the chair, the black eyes staring directly into the eye of the camera. "This is me," he seems to be saying. "All of this is me. Take it or leave it."

⚬⚭ 6 ⚬⚭

I walk on stilts down the entrance ramp to Interstate 80 heading east. I see the signs for Cheyenne, Omaha, Davenport, Chicago, Toledo, Boston. I can keep up with the cars on my stilts. It's a gift. Large faces without bodies line the south side of the highway. They are there to cheer for me, because I'm so fast on my stilts. Aunt Libby waves to me from the sidelines and chants my name: Susan, Susan, Susan.

As I walk, the stilts grow higher—about three stories—above the cars and then higher still. I am exhilarated at first. I am elated until I look down at the cars, which are as tiny as toys. I am moving too fast onto the highway and feel out of control with these long stilts. The principle is the same, I think, but the height panics me. I turn to call to Aunt Libby far below me.

"These stilts are too high," I shout.

She can't hear me. I can read her lips. She is calling my name and clapping her hands.

"How will I get down?" I am screaming. I can only imagine smashing my face on the asphalt.

The overhead light was on, but the house was silent. My skirt twisted around my hips, and a tight rubber band cut into my chest.

I still wore my shoes, which now seemed to be attached to wooden feet. On the desk the red digital clock read 3:00 A.M.

Do dreams foretell the future?

Mentally I listed my own future: graduate from high school in a month. Work at the market and paint over the summer. Attend the university in the fall. Major in art and minor in education. Teach art in high school. Get married. Have children. Die.

The exhilaration was missing. The anxiety of being on high, head-in-the-cloud stilts was missing. The applause was missing.

I tried again: graduate from high school in a month. Work at the market and paint over the summer. Attend the university in the fall. Major in art. Be a painter. Die.

Again: graduate from high school in a month. I imagined myself on stilts, moving through traffic. Graduate from high school in a month and—Cheyenne, Omaha, Davenport, Chicago, Toledo, Boston. I wanted the exhilaration, the anxiety, the applause.

I wanted to leave home.

Why hadn't I thought of it before? I was old enough now. I wanted to graduate from high school and leave. I didn't want to be here another four years while I went to college. Away from home I could be a painter and paint what I needed to paint without creating a constant upheaval in my family. I was old enough. I could leave home. And Aunt Libby was the key. Aunt Libby.

I literally leapt out of bed and pulled off my skirt and blouse, twirled about the room in my underwear, waving paintbrushes and singing softly, "I'm gonna live, live, live before I die." I caught sight of my face in the mirror above the dresser drawers and stood still. It was a young face, flushed, almost pretty. I leaned into the mirror.

"I'm going to Boston to live my life as a painter," I said to my reflection. "Do you hear me?" I asked. "I'm going to have a life. My life. I'm going to be an artist." I stared into my eyes, which were as blue as Willy's used to be. "I'm coming, Boston." And then I kissed my reflection in the mirror.

Terrific decisions can't wait. I had to act right then, so I put on my robe and burst into the living room, where Libby slept on the Hide-A-Bed.

Her disheveled head shot up from the pillow, her face startled until she recognized me. "You scared the liver out of me," she said.

"Sorry," I said. "I have something important to ask you."

"What time is it?" she asked.

I looked at the clock above the dining room table. "Three thirty."

"A.M.?"

"Yes."

"Come back at nine." She covered her head with the quilt.

I pulled the quilt back. "No, this can't wait. Please," I pleaded.

She lifted herself up enough to lean on her elbows. "I was up until two talking with your mother," she said. "That was only a short hour and a half ago. I'm on vacation, you know."

"I know. Sorry. It's just that I got this idea, and I won't be able to do anything else until I talk to you about it. I mean . . ."

She smiled. It seemed like a good sign.

"I—I want to come to Boston." I just spit it out. "I wondered if you'd put me up—just for the summer." I wanted to stay for the rest of my life, but I didn't think now was the time to tell Libby that. "I wouldn't be any bother. I could take care of myself and get a job and—"

"It's a good idea."

"I can do the cooking and the washing. I'd be a regular slave, and you'd never know I was around, except—what?"

"I said, I think it's a good idea," she said. "I asked your mother last night if you couldn't come and stay with me for a while." She sat up completely, leaning against the back of the couch, the sheet pulled up over her chest.

"You did?" I was hunched on both knees on her mattress and began bouncing. "What did she say? Did she say yes?"

"She didn't say no. She wanted to talk to your father first of course."

"Of course," I said, bouncing. "But what do you think? I mean, do you think it's promising?"

"She said the airfare could be your high school graduation present." Libby moved the sheet up to her throat. "I'll throw up if you don't stop wobbling the mattress," she said.

"Sorry." I let out a little screech. "I'm so excited. I can't stand it. Just a few minutes ago I was thinking how boring my life was—I had this dream about being up on stilts." I told her the dream.

"Maybe it was a warning dream," she said.

"No, it was a dream of possibilities."

"It sounds like an anxiety dream to me."

"I know, but what's the point in living if there's no anxiety? It means you're not testing yourself. You're not doing anything hard. Besides, for a while it was so exhilarating to be way up high in the sky. Before I looked down, it was so good."

Libby studied my face. "You'll have to sleep on my screened porch, you know. That's all I have besides my bedroom, which is tiny, but I used to sleep there in the summer myself. It's not that bad."

"It'll be perfect," I said.

"Have you got a slide portfolio of all your work?" she asked.

"I'm in the process of putting it together. Mr. Tuttle, my art teacher, is helping me."

She nodded in approval. "Lots of galleries in the Boston area. "You'll want to make the rounds."

"I know," I said. "I'll bring the paintings too. I can talk Daddy into making a crate to carry them."

She yawned. "Get out of here now and let me sleep." She slithered back down under the blankets and covered her head with the pillow.

"Okay, I'm going. See, I'm going. I'm standing up now. I'm

tiptoeing around the bed. Whoops, I'm back on the bed and bouncing again!" The whole Hide-A-Bed squeaked and groaned.

Libby swung a pillow at me. "Get off my bed." She couldn't help laughing, though.

"I'm really leaving now," I said. *I'm going to Boston, I'm going to Boston,* I sang in my head. I knew it would happen. You can just feel those things.

Knowing I wouldn't be able to sleep, I put on my sweats and ran to the museum through backyards and alleys and then stood in the bushes with my nose pressed against the window to see if I could see my painting in the semidarkness. I could only see the dark shape of it. This was my real home, this museum with its paintings of landscapes I knew well: Spanish Fork and American Fork Canyons, Lamb's Canyon, and Utah Lake. Even though the painters, John Hafen, Florence Ware, Waldo Midgley, and LeConte Stewart, were now long dead, their visions remained. From the steps I watched the sky grow lighter, tapping my foot to the music in my head, and followed a garbage truck making its way down the street, the two men in the back emptying overflowing cans into the maw of the truck. Art City was waking up. I walked slowly toward Fiona's house to tell her my news.

I'm sure Marianne had no idea how strange it would be to have her wedding reception in the Springville Museum when she booked it months before. The wedding line actually stood directly in front of my painting. People commented on it to Mother and me as they passed through the line. "Yes, isn't it a wonderful coincidence?" Mother would say, smiling. We had made up, in a curious sort of way. She just started speaking to me again and made my favorite lemon squares the afternoon after the All High School Art Show. Probably Libby's being in the house had something to do with it. I don't know. Anyway, we never spoke about the painting. She never congratulated me for winning the Master's Award, and I could never bring myself to say that I was sorry for painting the portrait, because I really wasn't, although I was sorry that it hurt her as much as it did. Perhaps I should have said that much. I don't think either one of us wanted to talk about it at all.

I liked the wedding reception: the string orchestra in the far corner, the round refreshment tables with the lace cloths and the punch bowl that spurted pink punch from these little holes like a fountain. I noticed Derriere pushing his index finger onto one of the holes before my dad grabbed him and jerked him away from the table. I liked dancing in my pink gown with Heber and Dad and Grandpa and even Derriere. I liked standing arm-in-arm with Fiona out in the foyer while her dad took our picture. I liked all those high school paintings copied from the *National Geographic*s past and present, peering out at us from the walls. More than anything, I loved the Springville Museum itself with its brown-tiled floors, its tall windows and high ceilings.

I was filled with gladness because I was going to Boston and maybe Willy was there. Libby said she thought she'd seen him in Harvard Square.

I was getting up on those stilts: I was leaving home. I was going to be an artist.

❧❧

Boston, Massachusetts 02108

❧❧

𝟣

I sing a song of Boston. I sing her streets: Tremont, Newbury, Boyl-ston, Mt. Vernon, and Pinckney. I sing Commonwealth Avenue and Fenway Drive, Beacon Hill and Bunker Hill. I sing Trinity Church and King's Chapel, Faneuil Hall, Quincy Market, gaslights, Durgin Park and Union Oyster House. I sing the Mystic River Bridge, the Esplanade and the Boston Pops. I sing of swan boats, tea parties, and lunch at the Ritz. I sing Boston's names: the Adamses, the Kennedys, the Saltonstalls, the Lowells, the Cabots, Jordan Marsh and Filene's. I sing the Atlantic Ocean, the Celtics and the Red Sox. I sing Isabella Stewart Gardner.

I soar.
I fly over Boston.
I sing.

Libby greeted me with a bouquet of exploding irises just outside the jetway in Logan Airport. "These are for you," she said after we hugged. "Welcome to Boston."

"Oh, how perfect," I gushed. "No one has ever given me flowers before. Thank you."

She took my arm and led me through the corridor toward the baggage claim area. Logan Airport was older, shabbier than the Salt Lake Airport. It smelled like giant hot pretzels and sweat. I stared into faces of ethnic backgrounds I couldn't recognize. I was on a different planet, strange and wonderful. "I'm going to love it here," I said.

"It gets even better *outside* the airport." Libby laughed. We rode the escalator down. "Did you bring slides of your paintings to show around?" she asked.

"I brought all of them. I also brought most of the paintings. Dad made a wooden box for them. It looks like I brought a bed with me."

"Maybe you'll sell a painting or two this summer," she said.

We stood waiting for the luggage to spill into the carousel. The possibilities of the coming summer made me so immensely happy that I felt like I was going to float away, like gravity wasn't enough to keep my feet firmly planted.

"Meanwhile you'll probably want some kind of part-time job." Libby offered me a wrapped chocolate mint from her bag. I took it.

"I have to work," I said. "I have to support myself." I liked the sound of it. I was a responsible person—an adult.

"Well, I have a lead—you don't need to take it if you don't want to—but one of the secretaries in my office has a brother who manages a movie theater in Boston, and he's looking for a part-time person to sell candy—about twenty to thirty hours a week."

"Really? I'll do anything."

Libby pointed at the luggage now moving around the carousel. "I have his name and number at home. You can give him a call in the morning if you want to. I'm sure there are other things around."

Libby and I carried the luggage to her tiny Toyota, with a skycap following close behind, wheeling a crate of paintings on a cart. She collapsed the backseat of the car to make room for all my paraphernalia. She and the skycap struggled to fit the luggage and the crate into the small space. I stood hugging the irises to my chest, taking deep breaths of Boston's sultry June air.

Soon we were driving through the dank Sumner Tunnel, water trickling down its tiled walls.

"We're under the harbor, you know," Libby said.

I tried not to imagine the walls caving in with the pressure of the seawater—the two of us drowning in Boston Harbor, but I thought of nothing else until we were free of the tunnel. We worked through a cement maze of highways following signs for Storrow Drive. Crowded buildings with slanted rooftops and billboards sped by. There wasn't a single mountain to be seen anywhere. Libby zipped in and out of traffic at an alarming speed. The Charles River, glistening blue, opened up on our right with dozens of white sailboats skimming its surface like water flies. A train moved swiftly across a bridge and disappeared into a hole.

"That's the Cambridge line. Takes you directly to Harvard Square in about five minutes from Charles Street."

The car lurched suddenly onto an exit, and within a few blocks we were in the most wonderful neighborhood of cobbled streets and sidewalks. Dark red brick rowhouses lined the narrow streets, their windows framed with black or green shutters and window boxes filled with petunias and spidery ferns that blew softly in the city winds.

"It's too beautiful," I said. "It's—"

"Art City!" Libby shouted.

"No, it's not. Where's the roller-skating rink?"

"That's it." She pointed to a large building across from a park.

I stuck my head out the open window and squinted up at the gold dome. "That's the statehouse," I said proudly. "I've seen it in a book."

"Smarty."

We turned into Charles Street with its tiny shops and art galleries. There wasn't a neon light anywhere to be seen. Driving slowly up Mt. Vernon Street, Libby muttered, "We'll never find a parking place at this time of day."

"You live on this street? I would give my whole life to live here,"
I said.

"I have." She smiled and stopped the car. "Ask that guy if he's
coming out." A man was placing an old chair into the trunk of his
car.

"Excuse me," I said politely.

"Are you leaving?" Libby roared over my shoulder.

The man nodded. "But I have to get two more chairs."

He had to walk a fourth of the way down the block to get the
chairs.

"Aren't there other parking places?" I asked meekly.

"Not right in front of my building. This is so incredibly lucky,"
she said.

"Don't you have a garage?"

Libby guffawed. "Only if you're a billionaire. I make very good
money and I spend most of it to live in a small apartment on this
street."

"It's worth it," I said, admiring the exquisite rowhouses.

"I think so too," she said. Libby's building had a patch of grass in
front of it and an iron fence around it. Black pots of geraniums
edged the wide stairway to the front door. I would do a watercolor
of the doorway. Just the doorway.

The man had loaded the three chairs into his car, tied the trunk
down with a rope, and was now inching his way out of the parking
space. Another car was making its way down the street behind us.
"Get out quick and stand by our parking place. She'll nose into it
front-first if you don't."

"Huh?" was all I could say.

"Go save our parking place," she yelled.

I opened the door warily, laid the iris on the front seat, and got
out. I really didn't understand my function standing there in the
middle of this narrow street in Boston. I mean, everyone knows
that if you're parallel parking, you back into it, you don't come into
it front-first. It was obvious, to anyone who could see, that Libby

was going to back into that parking place. Then the little black BMW nosed its front into Libby's parking place as the other car pulled out around Libby. Evidently the rules were different in Boston. Whoever got in first was the winner.

I stood directly in front of the car. "This is our parking place," I said firmly. I added "ma'am," when I saw that the woman was much older than me. My mother wouldn't think it was respectful to have a confrontation with an older person.

The driver stuck her head out of the car. "Says who?"

"I do, ma'am," I said. "We've been waiting ten minutes for this space."

"Move aside, or I'll run over you."

"That's what you'll have to do," I said, swallowing hard.

The woman rolled her car forward a few inches. I placed my hands on the hood of her car.

"Back off, you buffalo cow," Libby roared from the front seat of her car. She had backed the Toyota into the parking space so that her back bumper touched the back of my leg, while the other car's front bumper touched the front. I stood squeezed between them. The woman called Libby the A-word preceded by the F-word. In Springville, Utah, you never hear a middle-aged woman dressed respectably, as this woman was, yelling the A-word and the F-word like that, so this was a first for me.

"This is our space," I said again. My voice sounded more like a bleat than a voice.

The woman said I should do something to myself that was, practically speaking, impossible. She used the S-word again and again and then lay on her horn. Libby shouted the S-word back, along with unspeakable buffalo acts and honked her horn as well. Together they shouted a whole alphabet of obscenities at each other. I tried not to blush, since no one else did, but my face was blazing. I was sure of it.

Then both women moved their cars just a millimeter or so. I hollered my head off. "My legs, my legs!" And collapsed forward onto the hood of the BMW. I saw the shocked expression on the woman's face. She backed the car out of the space, and I crumpled down onto the curb and rubbed my shins, which were going to be black and blue for sure.

"Are you all right?" the woman asked, breathless. She and Libby now both hovered over me.

"You were going to break my legs over a parking space!" I said. I hated both of them.

"I'm sorry. I didn't think that—"

"It was our space," Libby said.

"You were going to break my legs—" I looked at Libby.

"It's so hard to find a parking space," the woman moaned.

"It's impossible," Libby agreed.

"I can't believe this. You were going to break my legs over a parking space!" I shouted at them.

"I guess we were," the woman said.

Another car had now moved down the street and was blocked behind the BMW. The man rolled down his window. "Is that space available?" he asked.

Libby and the woman both laughed. "It definitely isn't," the woman shouted. "You're all right, aren't you?" she asked me.

"I am," I said, still rubbing my shins.

"I'd better move my car, then." She went back to her car, pulled around Libby, and actually waved to us as she drove down the street. *Welcome to Boston,* I thought to myself.

I stood on the sidewalk while Libby parked. As I gathered the irises from the front seat and Libby opened the trunk of the car, a man wearing a sweat suit came out of the apartment building, smiling out of the side of his mouth. "I heard your arrival," he said to Libby, who was bent over the trunk. He was quite good-looking in a Clark Kent sort of way. I liked his glasses. "As a matter of fact I think the entire building heard your arrival."

"Why didn't you come out and help then?" Libby said sourly, placing the two suitcases on the sidewalk.

"You obviously didn't need help." He reached down to pick up the luggage.

"Not those, take this crate of paintings," Libby ordered.

The man stood straight at attention and clicked his Nikes together. "Yes, sir—I mean, ma'am. I mean General Schroeder, *ma'am!*" He saluted.

I laughed out loud. Libby's shoulders slumped, and she pushed her head into the man's chest. "Sorry—I forgot myself. Forgive me. I'm so shovey."

"Once a general, always a general. It must be all that Germanic blood coursing through your veins." He grinned at her. He had the warmest eyes.

"I almost forgot." Libby straightened up. "Meet my niece. This is Sue Smith. Sue, this is Dan Lavenstein. He lives downstairs from me."

"Hi, Sue." Dan adjusted his glasses and smiled at me.

"Spelled with a five." I hadn't meant to say that. I had planned to leave the silent five behind in Springville, Utah, along with my adolescence, but it slipped out. I had to look up to see him, and the sun streamed past his ear, hitting me directly in the face. I shaded my eyes with my hand.

"A silent five," Libby said.

I nodded, squinting into his face. "I collect silences," I said.

"Like P. G. Wodehouse." He could tell I didn't know what he was talking about. "He wrote a book called *Leave It to Psmith,* and Psmith begins with a silent *P,*" he explained. "A British writer— dead now." He picked up the crate of paintings, and Libby and I followed behind into the apartment building. I would have to check out this P. G. Wodehouse guy.

"Susan is the artist I was telling you about," Libby said. I liked the sound of it, the way she said it, like she took me seriously.

"The elevator's broken again, so we'll have to take the stairs," Dan said, still leading the way.

"Sorry to say, we're on the fourth floor," Libby apologized to me.

A faint smell of onion permeated the hallway.

Dan stopped at the top of the stairs, his head craned awkwardly around the corner.

"Is she out?" Libby asked in a whisper.

"No." Dan just mouthed the word.

"Is who out?" I whispered, because they were whispering.

Libby cautioned me with an index finger. We moved quietly along the wide, carpeted hallway.

A stout old woman squeezed out of door number 10, barely opening it. "You're back!" she shouted. She held a small, white, furry dog, who licked her face as she talked. "Is this your niece?" Her gravelly voice boomed through the hallway. She looked me up and down.

Libby sighed heavily, and I thought Dan grunted. "Yes," she said. "Grace McGregor, I'd like you to meet—"

"I'm Constantinople Smith," I finished. New town, new name, I thought.

Grace McGregor eyed me suspiciously. "Wasn't that the name of a city?" She had the jowls of a bulldog.

"Yes, but now it's Istanbul—in Turkey," I said. "I was born there."

Libby snorted as she unlocked the door to her apartment. Dan stood behind her, grinning out of the side of his mouth.

"I was born in Hudson, Wisconsin, but my parents didn't call me Hudson, thank the Lord." She kissed the dog on his lipless mouth. I wanted to gag. "Wouldn't that be something?" she addressed the dog. "If I were named Hudson McGregor? I'm a Lutheran," she said.

Libby and Dan had disappeared into Libby's apartment. The door stood wide open.

"Nice to meet you." I nodded politely and took a few more steps. Grace McGregor followed right behind.

"This is Priceless." She shoved the dog into my arm, so I was compelled to turn back and give it a little pat on the head. Priceless licked my finger. "It's a nice dog," I lied. I hated licking dogs. I turned to leave her again.

"He's twelve years old. I don't know what I'll do when he dies."

"Maybe he won't die," I said, trying to inch my way down the hall.

"Everything dies," she said.

Not soon enough, I thought.

"He's so priceless." She and the dog smooched again. Grace held my arm with her free hand. "Do you want to see him do his tricks? He can jump through the hoop and play dead."

I was trapped, helpless.

"Not now, Grace," Libby bellowed from her doorway. "Sue, I mean, Constantinople will have to see it later. She's had a long trip, and she needs to eat her dinner." She pulled me into the apartment and shut the door right in Grace McGregor's tired old face.

Libby snickered at what must have been my shocked expression. "You're going to have to learn to get away from her," she said, "or you'll spend the whole summer in that hallway." We were standing in a narrow corridor lined with etchings in black frames. An oriental carpet covered part of the wooden floor. I followed her, catching a glimpse of the living room on one side and a bedroom on the other. The corridor ended in a large kitchen with black-and-white tiles on the floor. Dan leaned against an old wooden table with a black marble top in the center of the room. My luggage and packages were heaped at his feet. The late-afternoon sun flowed in a single shaft of light through a small irregular window near the ceiling.

"Looks like a Vermeer painting," I said. The room had a nice glow about it that I liked.

Libby laughed. "Don't tell the landlord that. He'll raise the rent."

"Are these your paintings, Constantinople?" Dan asked, emphasizing the name. He had this half grin out of the side of his mouth.

"Sue Smith is such a boring name," I explained.

"Even with a five in it?"

I nodded.

"I want to see your paintings before I go." He used a claw hammer to break open the crate. Libby removed the pads. I set the various canvases against the cupboards lining the kitchen. Dan stared at them for what seemed to be a millennium. I began swallowing, even though there wasn't any spit in my mouth.

"These are good," he said finally. "They're really good. How old are you anyway?"

"Almost eighteen," I said.

"Incredible," he said. He stared at the Anasazi woman and her baby.

"Do you think she's a possibility? I mean, is she good enough?" Libby asked him.

"They certainly look good to me," he said. He grasped my hand. "Nice to meet you, Susan Smith with the silent five. Welcome to Bean Town."

"Thanks," I said.

He squeezed Libby's hand. "See ya tomorrow, Lib," he said. He grinned out of the side of his mouth again and let himself out of the door. "Can't talk now, Grace," we heard him shout from the other side of the door.

I could have sworn that Libby never mentioned Dan Lavenstein's name in Utah. He was clearly more than just a friend. I could tell from the kind of eyeball communication that existed between the two of them, the way he put his hand on the small of her back at certain moments and the way she leaned into him, that there was more there. And it wasn't new. They weren't like Marianne and Heber, you know, kissing and hugging all the time, because being together was so new for the two of them. It was like they were married.

2

A large screened porch in back of the kitchen was to be my bedroom. It was literally sitting in two large elm trees that grew out of almost no dirt that I could see at the back of the apartment building. Through the branches and around them were more red brick buildings and rooftops, and at one certain angle I could catch a glimpse of the Charles River if I stood on my toes. There were no mountains, which was fine with me.

"If it gets cold out here, you can come in and sleep on the couch," Libby told me. "But it should stay fairly hot now," she said.

There was an iron bed covered with an old quilt against the inside wall, a chest of drawers with a mirror above it, a large wooden table with a chair, and a rattan rocker with another blanket draped over one arm.

"I used to sleep here in the summers. It's cooler," Libby said. "This year I finally bought an air conditioner for my bedroom."

"It's perfect," I said. "It's all I need." I set my easel in a corner next to the table and sat on the bed.

Libby helped me put away my clothes, and we left to go to dinner. Grace McGregor was not in the hallway. "Thank heaven we don't have to plow through that old bat," Libby muttered as we made our way down the stairs.

We ate at the Union Oyster House, where I had oysters on the half shell for the first time in my life. I was determined to like them, and I did, especially with plenty of that red seafood sauce that comes with them. I also ate my first lobster. It was celestial— food for the gods—and I moaned while I ate until Libby began imitating me, and we both burst into laughter. Libby was nothing like a parent. "You're not making me eat any vegetables," I couldn't help saying. "I like it."

"I'm not going to be your mother this summer," she said, sucking meat out of the lobster's legs. I had given up on finding any more meat. "For one thing," Libby continued, "I'm not good at it. You'll have to be responsible for yourself, your own meals, your laundry—everything. My job is very demanding, and I often have to leave early and come home late."

"We'll be like roommates," I said.

She nodded. "We'll *have* to be roommates. I'm a terrible care-taker. As a matter of fact I used to wonder if I could take care of anyone—really worried about it. I've lived alone since college."

"I'd like living alone," I said, propping myself on one elbow.

She laid the lobster aside and wiped her mouth with her napkin. "You probably *would* like living alone," she said. "Still, I always wondered if I could care for someone or even something." She began laughing. "A few years ago"— she stopped to laugh again— "I bought these goldfish and kept them in a bowl in the kitchen." She lowered her voice to a whisper. "I *resented* having to feed them. They all died of starvation!" She covered her face with her hands briefly as if she was truly embarrassed. "Can you believe it?" she said.

To tell the truth, it was hard to believe. I mean, how hard is it to sprinkle food into a goldfish bowl once a day? All I said was, "I see your point. I'm tired of being overfed and fretted about anyway. Between Mother and Grandma, I sometimes feel like I'm suffocating. I can take care of myself. Besides," I said, "I don't want to be found floating limply at the top of the fishbowl at the end of the summer."

Libby laughed. "We'll get along fine, then. Come on, let's go for a walk." She paid the check, and we began our walk through the Haymarket.

Most of the shops were closing, so we gazed leisurely into windows and spent pretend money extravagantly and even kept track, so that by the time we were finished, we had spent over $100,000 apiece. One of my favorite "acquisitions" was a seven-foot-tall papier-mâché giraffe. I thought it would look wonderful peeking over my easel while I worked. Libby said it was a good night's work. We bought frozen-yogurt cones and sat under a lamp on a bench eating them. I wanted to ask Libby about seeing Willy, but I didn't dare. She would want to know why I was so curious.

When we got home, I walked around Libby's apartment and inspected the graphics she had hanging on the walls. "Are any of these yours?" I asked her. She was in the kitchen, and I stood out in the hall.

"The ones that aren't signed," she said. "The terrible ones. The rest of them are done by people I was in art school with. We used to trade prints."

"I really like this one of the woman in the bathing suit with the shells around her feet," I said.

"Thanks," Libby yelled from the kitchen.

"What have you done lately?" I asked, standing in the doorway of the kitchen, where she was emptying the dishwasher.

"Nothing you could hang on a wall, believe me." She placed some glasses into a cupboard just above her head. "I'm an executive art director for an advertising agency, but my work is primarily administrative. I don't do actual artwork anymore, although I began as a commercial artist. I used to draw the interior of airplanes." She laughed.

I made a face. "I'd hate that," I said.

"I was glad to have a job drawing anything and getting paid for it." She shut the dishwasher door and leaned against the counter, her hands tucked into the front pockets of an apron that looked as if it had been sewn out of the British flag. My face must have looked disapproving, because she said, "You think what I do is a kind of sellout, don't you?"

"No, I really don't. It's just that I've never thought of being a commercial artist. It's never entered my mind. I'm a little surprised now that it hasn't, but I've always wanted only to paint people and the ideas I have about them."

She nodded and stared at my paintings, which were still displayed along the edge of the kitchen cupboards. They looked extraordinarily rich after looking at Libby's graphics. "I suspect," Libby sighed, "that you'll be able to paint what you want and make money too." She yawned suddenly. "And if I don't go to bed right away, I won't be able to get to work in the morning, and I'll be hoping for some job selling popcorn in a movie theater." She turned off the kitchen light. A warm glow of light came from the screen porch and the hallway.

"Thanks for everything," I said.

"You're entirely welcome. Good night, Susan Smith with the five in your name."

"Good night, Aunt Susan Elizabeth Schroeder."

"Who on earth is that?" Libby laughed, padding down the hall in her bare feet.

I lay on my bed in the trees of Beacon Hill and listened to the traffic of nearby streets. It seemed kind of odd to me that all my life I had thought of Libby as an artist—a fine artist like me—but she was really an executive. Funny how you get those ideas about people and they just sort of stick.

The next morning I met Grace McGregor in the hall again. She waited for me just outside Libby's door, holding Priceless and a large quilting hoop. Grandma used hoops sometimes when she wanted to quilt in her lap instead of sitting at a large frame in the basement, where it was too damp.

"Listen, Connie, do you have a minute right now? I want to show you how good Priceless is at doing tricks." She paused to squeeze and kiss Priceless, who sat contented in the fat crevice of her arm. "You don't mind if I call you Connie, do you? Constantinople is such a mouthful. I told Priceless last night that I thought I'd call you Connie. I'll bet your mother calls you Connie too, doesn't she?" She snuggled Priceless and adjusted the hoop on her other arm.

"My mom calls me Sue. Why don't you call me Sue too?" I felt bad about lying to her.

"Sue? That doesn't sound like a nickname for Constantinople. What do you think, Priceless?"

I expected Priceless to talk back for a brief moment. "Actually I was joking yesterday. My name isn't Constantinople. It's Susan or Sue." I was sorry I had lied to her. She looked so vulnerable. Her body was bagged in wrinkles.

She stared at me hard. She seemed to have nothing to say about my confession. "Wellll," she drawled finally. "My name isn't Grace either." She laughed in a gravelly laugh. "It's actually Lucinda May Hollingsworth Santiago McGregor. I was married twice." Her cheek rested against Priceless's face. She smiled benignly at me.

"You're kidding," I said, but I wasn't sure. "Everyone—Dan and Libby—call you Grace," I stammered.

"I've been lying for years," she whispered. She leaned forward just inches from my face. "So you and I have a lot in common, don't we?"

I stepped back. "I'm going to call you Grace," I said decisively.

She clapped her hands, almost dropping Priceless in the process. "Good idea," she laughed. "Because that's my name. We tricked her, didn't we Priceless? We tricked Miss Smarty here for a brief second. Yes, we did. Jump down now, Priceless. Now it's your turn to do the tricks. Jump!" Priceless jumped lightly to the floor and sat on his hind legs, begging. Grace shook an index finger at him. "Not until you jump through the hoop. Jump!" she commanded, holding the quilting hoop a foot and a half above the ground. "Jump, Priceless, jump!"

Priceless jumped through the hoop and back again. Grace hollered with delight, both arms stretched above her head as if she had just completed a marvelous feat in a circus arena. "Hurrah! What a good baby," she squealed. She fed him a mouthful of chocolate-covered raisins that she took out of the pocket of her dress.

"That's a good trick, all right," I said, clapping politely. I hoped she would offer me some of the chocolate-covered raisins, but she didn't. Instead she held some of them in her hand above her head. "Jump for it, Priceless!" she commanded.

The dog made a few effortless low leaps into the air. "Higher!" Grace screeched. She shook the fist of raisins high above the animal's head. "Jump higher!"

The dog danced and circled below her hand on his hind legs, his nose reaching in the air, and then suddenly leapt several feet, actually touching Grace's hand.

"Hey, that's quite good," I said. I really hadn't thought that such a tiny dog could jump that high.

Grace danced in a circle, Priceless running and yapping about her feet. She offered him more chocolate raisins. "What a precious, priceless dog you are." She bent over, cooing. "Now play dead," she said.

I began to wonder how many tricks Priceless had in his repertoire. I had called Mr. Zaccardi at the Bijou movie theater, and he had told me to come right then if I could. He would be waiting for me. "I have to go pretty soon," I said, watching Priceless turn limp on the floor. He lay on his back, his head twisted to one side, his mouth open, his eyes closed. "Very good," I said. I looked at my watch. Half the morning was practically over.

"Shhh, Priceless is dead. Shhh." The dog twitched slightly.

Grace touched his stomach lightly, and he jumped nervously out of his feigned sleep. "Through the hoop," she shouted. The dog jumped back and forth through the hoop. Grace threw the hoop down and made a hoop of her arms. "Through my arms," she commanded. He jumped back and forth. "Now jump high." He leapt on the first try.

I hoped this was the finale. "I've really got to go," I said, moving toward the stairwell.

"Kill, Priceless, KILL!" Grace's extended arm pointed at me. The flesh under her upper arm flapped back and forth. "KILL," she commanded.

Priceless bared his tiny teeth and growled and snarled around my feet. I tried to back away. He followed energetically, nipping at my shoe. "Hey," I cried out.

Grace began to laugh. "Come to Mama," she said to the dog. Priceless jumped into her arms and licked her face and ear. "Better not tell any more lies, Miss Constantinople Susan Smith, or you'll get eaten by a four-pound dog." She petted the dog, turned her back on me, and disappeared behind her apartment door. I could still hear her laughing as I made my way down the stairs.

3

The Bijou was located on Washington Street, several blocks down from Jordan Marsh, New England's biggest department store, in the heart of downtown Boston. I could get there by walking to Charles Street, down past the statehouse, through the grassy Common, across Tremont and over a block. Grandma Smith would have thought Washington Street was "sleazy." She would have used that exact word. It *was* crowded and dirty, the buildings undistinguished, and it had an overabundance of movie theaters and narrow alleys where, I imagined, derelicts lived. I liked it. I liked the density, the play of shadow and light across the brick and concrete. I liked the energy of the people who passed by on the sidewalk.

I don't think the guy who managed the theater, Salvatore Zaccardi, knew anything about interviewing people for a job, even though he did have this clipboard with yellow paper and a ballpoint pen with BIJOU monogrammed in gold on it. I mean, he just set me down on this crummy, soiled sofa in the lobby and told me the story of his life, all the time tapping the pen against the clipboard. He said he was twenty-eight and had never left the city of Boston except once, when he and his family vacationed in the Berkshires and he wheezed the whole time he was there. "Boston is the greatest city in the world, and there's no reason to go anywhere else," he told me in his thick Boston accent. "It's the Athens of America," he boasted. "You heard of the Boston Marathon?"

I nodded.

"This," he pointed his index finger at the floor, "this is where they have it."

"In this theater?"

"No, I mean in this very city."

"That must be why they call it the *Boston* Marathon," I said.

"Hey, you're sharp!" His eyebrows went up in surprise. "So, Susan, do they have movie theaters way out there in Utah?"

Something—a look in his eyes—made me answer, "No. We don't have television either, although I understand they have it in Ohio."

"No kidding."

"That's what I heard."

"So what do you do for fun *way out there*?" He was still playfully tapping his pen on the clipboard.

"At night we make camp by gathering the oxen and covered wagons into a circle." I sat forward on my seat. "Mother makes hoecakes for supper, and then all of us square-dance the night away to Grandpa Smith's banjo music."

He smiled placidly at me and nodded. "So," he paused. "Can you work a cash register?"

"I learned in my father's grocery store."

His head bobbed up and down. "Good, good," he said. "You want to see my family?" He was already pulling his wallet out of his back pocket.

I couldn't help smiling. The whole interview was idiotic. He took out a folded magazine page and carefully unfolded it, smoothing it against his chest. "You ready?" he asked, protecting the photograph against his body.

"Sure," I said, still smiling. This guy was a nut.

"Here they are." He turned the creased picture around for me to see. It was a full-page photograph of a mother gorilla and two baby gorillas. "This is my mom and this is my sister, Josie, and my brother, Tony."

I burst out laughing. "You look like your brother Tony," I said.

"Everyone says that," he said. "Of course, Josie got all the good looks in the family." He patted the picture with pretended affection and then folded it again.

"So, Susan," he said, placing his wallet into his back pocket. "You want to work here?"

"Yes," I said.

"When do you want to start?"

"As soon as possible."

He wrote something down on his clipboard. "I'm going to show you a figure," he said. "It's your hourly wages give or take a few zeros." He shoved the clipboard over to me to look at.

I began to laugh again. "Sixty thousand dollars an hour is just fine with me," I said.

"Good, then it's settled. I'll have to show this to the owner. He might want to play around with the zeros a little, but I think he'll go for it." He reached out and shook my hand. "Did anyone ever tell you that you have a funny accent?"

"You sound just like Peter Jennings," I said.

"Thanks," he said. Only it came out sounding like "tanks."

I stayed the rest of the afternoon at the Bijou working in the concession stand and wearing a red jacket and cap made of synthetic fibers. A girl named Zella with a bad complexion trained me. She said we were allowed free drinks, but if they caught us lifting any of the candy, we'd be fired instantly. She slashed her throat with her index finger to illustrate the gravity of the crime. I also met the tall, lanky usher, Sweeney, who blushed whenever I spoke to him. A middle-aged woman named Jill sold tickets in the front. I liked these people. I liked the elegant shabbiness of the Bijou Theater. I liked myself away from home.

*   *   *

I met Libby as I turned into Mt. Vernon Street. It was almost eight o'clock, and I was bushed. I could tell Libby was tired too, because she almost waddled up the sidewalk.

"Are you just getting home now?" she asked me.

"Yes. I'm a working girl at Boston's Bijou Theater. I brought you a treat." I handed her a giant box of buttered popcorn.

"Oh, terrific—dinner!" She opened it as we walked. "Congrats on the job. Did you meet Josie's brother?"

"Yes. His name is Salvatore. Can you believe it?"

Libby laughed. "What's he like?"

"He's crazy!" I told her about the interview and the picture of the gorillas.

"He's as bad as Josie. She really keeps the office jumping." We were now walking up the steps of the apartment. Libby stopped in the mailroom adjacent to the lobby to pick up her mail. I wished there was something for me, but I'd only been there a full day and knew that was impossible.

Grace lurked over us as we dragged ourselves up the stairs. "Here comes Libby and Sue, Priceless. Here they come. And look, they're eating popcorn! They're almost to the top of the stairs now. They're almost home."

As we approached the fourth-floor landing, Libby, much to my surprise, shoved Grace on the shoulder, just pushed her bodily away from us. "Back, Grace, back. We're too tired to talk."

The old lady was about to open her mouth.

"No, Grace, back, I say." Libby continued saying this as she pulled her keys out of her purse. "Don't talk, just stay away. I'm not in the mood."

Grace stood with her back to the wall, hugging Priceless, who was licking her face. "You are hurting Priceless's feelings," she said. "There's a little doggy tear on his face. Don't cry, Priceless. Poor Priceless," she cooed to the dog.

Inside the apartment Libby leaned against the door and sighed. "She drives me up the wall."

This wasn't the time to mention it, but I felt sorry for Grace McGregor.

"Why is she always out in the hall?" I asked.

Libby kicked off her shoes and collapsed onto the sofa in the living room. "Because there isn't any room in her apartment. She's a pack rat in the extreme." She shoved a handful of popcorn into her mouth. "Her place is loaded to the ceiling with junk. She hasn't thrown anything away in forty years or longer." She threw her arm across her eyes.

"What kind of junk?"

"Who knows? Old-lady junk: boxes of beer mats and pens and pencils and yarn in miscellaneous colors and cottage cheese cartons with their lids, rubber bands, magazines that haven't been in circulation for decades—I could go on and on." She peeked at me from under her arm and smiled wearily. "In fact I have gone on and on."

"Grandma Smith does that. Mother says she never throws anything away."

"No, it's not like Grandma Smith. She at least stores things in cupboards and closets or in the basement, but Grace has things stored to the ceiling, I mean literally to the ceiling throughout her whole apartment."

I had never heard of such a thing. "Her whole apartment?"

"Evidently she has narrow aisles through the collection of crap in every room. Her bed and a table are in the kitchen, and that's where she lives. I understand even the kitchen is beginning to fill up."

"Have you been in it?"

"No! She won't let you in. That's why she barely opens the door to come out. She doesn't want you to see it. Mrs. Whitten, downstairs, brought Grace food when she was sick once, and she said the whole apartment is stuffed full except for the kitchen, where Grace and that pain-in-the-behind dog of hers live."

"Why would anyone do that?"

Libby gathered herself into a fetal position, yawned, and closed her eyes. "Don't know. I can't stay awake. Let me snooze for a few minutes, okay?" She handed me the popcorn box. "Dinner," she said.

I took the rest of the popcorn and went into the kitchen and opened the refrigerator. It was almost completely empty except for some juice, some milk, a six-pack of Mountain Dew, and junk that you don't eat except in combination with other things. I was tired and starving. Rummaging through doors and cupboards I found a can of tuna fish and some white bread and made a toasted tuna fish sandwich. I sat alone at the table, eating and feeling disappointed that Libby was sleeping. I really wanted to talk more about Salvatore Zaccardi and my job at the Bijou. I wanted to know more about Grace McGregor and her strange habits.

I decided to call home. I stood next to the wall phone in the kitchen and waited for someone to pick up the phone *way out there* in Springville, Utah. On the fifth ring Derriere answered.

"Hi, it's me!" I said into the phone.

"It's Susan," he said to someone else in the room, probably my parents. "Are you in Boston?" he said to me.

"Yes, and it's great," I said. "What are you doing?" I could hear a noise in the background.

"We're eating dinner and watching *Wheel of Fortune,*" Derriere said.

"So late?"

"It's only six-fifteen," Derriere said.

"Oh, sure, the time difference. We're two hours ahead. What are you eating?"

"That spinach-and-rice casserole—ick."

My mouth watered. Spinach and rice is a favorite of mine. It's really a more-than-passable wilted-vegetable casserole. It has eggs and cheese and rosemary and thyme—

"And fried chicken," Derriere continued.

I wished I hadn't asked him. I could have eaten a buffalo.

"Susan?" Mother interrupted. "Are you all right? Why did you call?"

"I just wanted to tell you that I got a job," I said. "I sell candy in a movie theater right in the middle of Boston. It's just great," I said.

"How much are you making? Will you be able to save any money?"

I told her how much.

"Maybe you should open a savings account," she said anxiously. "Is the theater in a good neighborhood?"

"It's right downtown, Mother."

"You won't be working at night, will you?"

"It's a movie theater. Of course I'll be working some nights."

"How do you get to work? Does Libby take you?"

"I walk. It's only a mile from here."

"Don't walk alone at night. It's too dangerous." And then she must have turned to Dad, because she said in a completely altered voice, "What? She won eighteen thousand dollars? You're kidding. She has to pay the income tax, though. What would that come to?"

"Mother!" I called.

"Oh, I'm sorry. We were just watching this woman on *Wheel of Fortune,* and she's just won everything in sight."

"I'm going to take my portfolio to some galleries in Cambridge tomorrow. I'll ride the subway in—scary, huh?" I made this decision about the time I said it to her on the phone.

"Oh, my gosh, now she's going for a red Porsche."

"Mother!"

"I'm sorry," she apologized. "It's hard to get away from the television with it blaring in the same room."

"Go into the bedroom and use the phone, then."

"Honey, we can't talk that long. It's too expensive. Are you feeling all right? How did you like the plane ride? Does Libby live in a nice neighborhood?"

"She lives in the best neighborhood in America," I said.

"Is she taking good care of you? I mean, are you eating well and everything?"

I looked at the remaining part of the tuna fish sandwich lying forlornly on the kitchen table. "Of course," I said. "Mother, I really like Boston. It's the most beautiful city I've ever seen. You should see the architecture—"

"Your father wants to say hello before he goes back to the market. G'bye, hon."

"Susan, baby, how are you?" It was Dad's voice.

"Vanna! I hear you're really giving it away tonight."

"Yeah, wish I could get some of it for myself," he said. His voice sounded kind of weary. "You okay?"

"Yes. I really like it here. Boston is beautiful. I got a job. I ate lobster last night."

"Sounds like you're not feeling a whole lot of pain," he said. "I'm proud of you."

"Thanks, Dad,"

"It's 'fallen angel,'" he said louder.

"What?"

"Oh, sorry, Susan. It's the bonus round—it's 'fallen angel,' but I don't think she's going—she got it! That's the most money I've ever seen anyone win on *Wheel of Fortune*. Are you watching it, Susan?"

"No." I looked around the room. I hadn't even seen a TV in Libby's apartment. "Look, Dad, I'd better go."

"I'm glad you're enjoying yourself," he said. "Be a good girl,"

"I will. G'bye, Dad."

"Tell her not to come home!" Derriere repeated this in the background.

"'Bye, honey."

I stood still in the growing darkness of Libby's kitchen. The thought of my family watching *Wheel of Fortune* at home was depressing. The phone call hadn't satisfied me. I decided to call

Fiona. After a long wait and just as I was about to hang up, Fiona herself answered.

"Fiona? It's me in Boston." I had to work to keep my voice up.

"Fiver!" she exclaimed. Immediately I felt better. "How is it? You sound like you're just down the block."

"It's spectacular," I said. "I wish you were here." That was true enough. "You should see Libby's apartment!" I described the oriental carpets, the grand piano, the porcelain bowl with the dancing figures in relief on it. "She bought it in Paris," I breathed. "And she has two Chippendale side chairs that I've only seen in antique books; they must have cost a fortune." I spewed on about Beacon Hill and Salvatore and the lady with the BMW and Grace McGregor. Fiona interjected frequently with "cool" or "funny" or "wow."

"I feel so at home here," I confided. "I feel like I've come to my spiritual home. Does that sound too weird?"

Fiona said nothing.

"Are you there?" I asked.

"Yeah—I mean, no, that doesn't sound weird." Her voice had a funny catch in it. "Sue," she continued. She called me Sue only in her more serious moments; otherwise it was Fiver. "You're not coming home, are you?"

I'd almost forgotten how clever Fiona was, how well she knew me, how she sniffed things out. It was the Gypsy in her. It was why we were best friends.

"I just now realized it," she said, and I could hear a tiny shock of recognition in her voice—"You're not coming home, ever."

"No, really; I mean, I can't afford it—you know that." I was stammering.

"You're not coming home." She repeated it as if she was getting used to the idea.

"I haven't even considered that," I said.

"B.S."

"Well, *considered* it, yes, but it seems unlikely that I'll be able to —there's my parents—"

"Double B.S."

"You see it in my aura?"

"Guess I'll have to find a new roommate for fall," she said.

"Whoa. Not quite yet. This is only the wishful-thinking stage. Don't throw me off yet."

Fiona seemed not to hear me. "It won't be the same, you know. You'll make new friends and I'll make new friends, and when we get together, we'll reminisce about what we used to do together. You'll say I was your best friend in high school, and it will all seem so far away. It already does."

This was too depressing. "Give me a break," I said. "I've been gone one day and you've turned me into past tense."

"Mark my words," she said in a lowered voice.

"Is this a Gypsy prophecy?"

"I have my powers."

"Baloney."

"Plus the fact that you're utterly predictable." And then she laughed as if she'd said the funniest thing in the world.

"Thanks loads."

We talked a few more minutes and then played the game we always played on the phone: "You hang up first," she said.

"No, you first."

"No, we'll count to three and both hang up."

"Okay."

We counted together: "One, two, three—" But neither one of us hung up, and we burst out laughing. "You didn't hang up," we said in unison. We repeated this game four or five times before we were finally able to quit and actually hang up.

The kitchen was completely dark now; only a soft, dusky light filtered through the windows and from the doorway leading to the back porch. I felt empty again. Long-distance phone calls, I realized, were not that satisfying. The cutoff was too abrupt. I thought about Fiona while I finished the other half of the tuna sandwich. Surely she and I could remain best friends, even if I did stay in Boston. The cutoff was too abrupt.

Libby remained sleeping, so I went off to my porch and sketched Grace McGregor's face alongside my own face.

The doorbell rang. I waited to see if Libby would answer it. Nothing. It rang again, followed by a low knock. I set my sketch pad down on the bed and padded quietly in bare feet past the living room to open the door.

Dan Lavenstein stood holding a huge plate of food.

"Libby asleep?" he whispered.

I nodded.

"She doesn't cook, you know. She doesn't even eat unless she's fed, and she doesn't feed anyone or anything else. You should see what happened to her goldfish."

"She told me about them."

"It's a famous Libby story." He smiled out of the side of his mouth. "I, on the other hand, do cook—Coquilles St. Jacques—scallops—for you. He handed me the plate.

"Thank you," I whispered. I felt really grateful.

"Enjoy, and I'll see you later," he said, moving away from the door.

"Wouldn't you like to come in?" I asked. "Libby said she was only going to sleep a few minutes."

"A few hours is more realistic." He smiled. "I'll come by later. Happy eating."

"Thanks again," I said. "I'll have Libby call you."

I was to realize over the next few weeks that this was to be the fabric of my life that summer, that when I was not working, I would have my dinner alone, because Libby was seldom home from work at dinnertime. And if she was home, she collapsed on the sofa taking "a short nap," which meant two hours at least.

Often there was very little if anything to eat in the kitchen, so that I would have to plan and shop for food and cook it myself. Libby ate her main meal out at lunch with clients.

The reward was that she always awoke around ten, ready to talk, listen, eat, walk, and explore until one in the morning.

❦ 4 ❧

In the morning I made up a list of galleries from the phone directory that I might visit. There were several in Cambridge, across the river from Boston, and I copied them first, figuring I could sort of look for Willy and galleries at the same time. Libby had said she had seen him in Harvard Square, not once but twice, so that had to be my best bet. I didn't have to go to work until five, so I spent the morning redrawing Grace and Priceless so that I could paint them later. I was drawn to Grace's eccentricity, which I believed was not due to her age or senility or anything like that. She had always been eccentric, even as a baby. I believed that it was a way she had of entertaining herself. She probably ate chocolate-covered raisins before she had teeth. Grace was just being herself. The more I drew her, the more I was sure of this. The act of drawing people teaches you about them. I have great faith in this, although I've never said it aloud to anyone.

After lunch I headed for the New World Gallery in Cambridge. The subway was no problem. After buying a couple of tokens from this fossilized man sitting in a cage, I moved through the turnstile and through a tunnel that ended in a platform marked Harvard Square, already crowded with people. I stood on the edge of the crowd, avoiding eye contact with anyone else, and concentrated on a bold sign telling me in no uncertain terms that I was not to *spit* in the subway. It hadn't even occurred to me to spit there. I'm not a spitter. But my mouth filled with water, and I had to keep swallowing. What would have prompted such a sign? Rivers of unlegislated spit, no doubt.

In the overcrowded train holding on to a rod above my head, my bottom pressed into an old woman's shopping bag, I looked around for Willy. Would he be glad to see me? Would he even remember me? "I am Marianne's niece," I would explain if he looked stumped. "You sent me an armadillo necklace for my eighth birthday." That's what I'd say and then lift the necklace away from my neck for him to see. He wouldn't likely forget someone he had once sent a necklace to. Not a real sterling-silver necklace.

I examined every male face. Not one of them looked remotely like Willy. Would I recognize *him*? This new anxiety made me clutch the rod overhead so tightly that my knuckles blanched. He could wear glasses now or have gone prematurely gray or gotten fat. I shuddered to think of the handsome Willy with his gut drooping over his belt. No, he would look the same. Maybe better.

Above the ground in Harvard Square I was immediately drawn to the open black iron gate that led into Harvard Yard. The lovely red brick buildings with gabled roofs rose above the surrounding wall, and I was tempted to go look at it and look for Willy, too, but I got hold of myself and walked up Massachusetts Avenue toward Central Square as my map indicated—to the New World Gallery.

It was closed. But it wasn't the gallery for me anyway. Painted in gold letters under the gallery name was the phrase, SPECIALIZING IN WESTERN ART. The window display had several paintings of cowboys riding horses and two bronze sculptures of cowboys roping steer. The paintings, with their backgrounds of mountains and sagebrush, looked all too familiar and gave me a suffocating feeling. I was a Western artist who didn't specialize in Western art. I crossed the New World Gallery off my list. I wanted to take one of the electric buses that kept passing by on the wide avenue and play like I was on vacation, but I knew that if I didn't get the paintings placed and if I didn't get someone interested in my art, I would have a hard time convincing my parents that there was any immediate future for me in Boston. They would want me to come home at the end of the summer. It would be no use explaining that this was my real home—my spiritual home.

The White Orchid Gallery was located in a two-story frame house on Mellon Street, and it was open. There was no one in the first room I entered, which was filled with seascapes, all obviously done by the same artist. They were pleasantly pastel and fairly boring, I thought. The second room contained paintings that seemed to me to copy Mondrian, but they lacked the dynamic tension of his work. I stood in front of a black-and-white-and-red triangle, waiting for someone to see me.

Finally a squarely built woman carrying a stack of folders, her hair stiff as a wire brush, stepped through the arched doorway. "Oh," she said, when she saw me. "I didn't hear anyone come in." Her voice was as deep as a man's, and I wondered for a minute if she wasn't a man in a skirt and jacket. We had a neighbor in Springville who liked to dress in his wife's clothes sometimes. Everybody knew Mr. Mulford. He was quite harmless.

"I was just looking. I hope it's all right," I said.

"That's why we're here. Have you seen the watercolors in here?" she asked, walking into a third room. Her crepe-soled shoes sounded like Velcro zippers as she walked across the hardwood floors.

"No," I said, following her.

She set the file folders on a desk and sat down. "Nice, aren't they?"

"Yes, they are," I said. I hadn't even looked at the watercolors. Now that she was there, I remembered why I had come and felt awkward. I stood in front of her desk.

"I'm an artist," I said. It sounded quite lame.

She looked up then and studied me. "Ahaaa," she said, as if she had already smelled it on my breath.

She shook my hand firmly. "Marian Laird," she said. Marian was also a man's name, I couldn't help thinking.

"I have some slides of my work . . ." I pulled the thin looseleaf out of the canvas bag and opened it up. It seemed quite meager suddenly. "If you have time . . ." I laid the slides in the plastic protectors on her desk.

She took some half-glasses out of her jacket pocket and slipped them on. "I prefer that artists *send* their slides," she said, but she was not unfriendly.

"The most recent ones are here," I said, pointing.

She unlatched the looseleaf binder, pulled out that page, turned around to the light table behind her, and laid the slides down on the glass surface and snapped on the light. She peered at the slides through her glasses, holding the sides of the frames as she looked. "Oh, you're a portrait painter." She sounded disappointed. "I don't generally handle portraits," she said, without looking up. "They don't sell well. People don't want to hang strangers on their walls." Her head moved closer to the slides. "They're good, though," she added.

"These won prizes at the Springville Museum Show." I pointed to the family portrait and my dad's portrait.

She looked puzzled. "You mean Spring*field,* don't you?"

"No, Springville. Springville, Utah," I explained.

"Ahaaa."

I hated those *ahaaa*s of hers. I felt like I'd just won the local crayon-coloring contest at the corner Texaco station.

"What kind of show?" she asked.

"It was the All High School Art Show," I said. "They have about a thousand entries from all around the state and they accept only about four hundred of them. From those they choose three Master's Awards. That's what these got."

She peered at them again, more closely. Then she pulled them out of the plastic protector. "I'd like to see them on the screen," she said. I followed her to the kitchen, where a slide projector and screen were set up in what must have been a breakfast room at one time. She inserted three slides. My father on the Wheaties box appeared first, larger than life.

"He's a grocer," I said.

She smiled faintly and pressed the button to the next slide. It was the family portrait. She leaned forward to have a better look. She said it again: "Ahaaa." But I liked the way she said it this time. It showed appreciation.

"It's my family," I said. "My extended family." Willy smiled at me from his triangle.

"Very nice," she said. "This is very nice. How old are you?" she asked unexpectedly.

I thought it required a lie, and lying always makes me hesitate. "Eighteen," I said. I would be in two months, so it wasn't much of a lie. I probably should have said twenty-three.

"Mmmm," she said. "How big is this?"

I told her.

"Mmmm," she said again. So far it was three *ahaaa*s to two *mmmm*s.

She pushed the button to the next portrait. It was *The Woman in the Straw Hat.* Her face was shaded by the wide brim of the hat, except where speckles of sun fell on her face through the patterned holes in the brim. The woman was actually Grandma.

"It makes me look like I have chicken pox," Grandma had said when I showed it to her.

"It's the sunlight," I had explained. "Slivers of sunlight."

"Looks more like liver spots," she had said.

So I had kept this painting and painted her carrying a basket of flowers from her garden instead. She liked it so much she hung it in her living room.

Now the painting of Grandma, the one I preferred, with the hat and the dappled sunlight, shone on this stranger's slide screen, and

I anticipated another *mmmm* from her. Instead she turned the machine off and replaced the slides into the plastic protectors. "You're good," she said, removing her glasses and stuffing them back into her pocket. "You're very good. But you haven't matured into the painter you're going to be yet. That *Family Portrait* is dynamite, but you need more like that. You need enough to fill up a room at least. These"—she swept her hand across my looseleaf—"don't stand up alongside it." She closed the looseleaf and handed it to me.

"But do you need a whole roomful? How about just showing the one if you like it and then next fall I'll bring you some more?" I felt a little desperate. I wasn't ready to be cut off yet.

"No, I organize my rooms thematically," she said. "But do come by next fall and show me what you've done over the summer." Her hand was in the small of my back, and I realized that I was ever so politely being shoved out the door.

"Thank you," I said quickly. "It was nice of you to look at them."

"My pleasure," she said.

And then I was out on the sidewalk, squinting into the sun and feeling bewildered. She had seemed so interested. That last *ahaaa* was filled with promise. What had gone wrong? What magic word had I forgotten to speak?

"I felt like I was so close—like if I had said the right word, she would have hung them all right then and there," I told Libby and Dan late that night after I got home from work. We sat around the kitchen table sipping iced tea and Mountain Dew and eating Pepperidge Farm cookies out of the sack. My paintings still leaned against the lower cupboards.

"She kept saying 'ahaaa' like I had something." I exaggerated the *ahaaa,* and Libby and Dan both smiled.

"Did you go anywhere else?" Dan asked.

"Yes, this place on Brattle Street, but the guy said he didn't look at unsolicited slides at all. He said he had *his* artists—like they were his slaves or something."

Libby smirked and stirred more sugar into her tea. "Well, that's three down and how many to go?" she asked.

"Hundreds," I said. I showed her the list I had made.

"You're not giving up, are you?" Dan asked.

"No, this is just first-day discouragement," I said.

"I think you did great," Libby said. "I can't imagine running around to galleries myself. It sounds too humiliating."

Dan gathered up our glasses, set them in the sink, and stood behind Libby's chair, gently massaging her neck and shoulders.

"That's one of my favorites," he said, pointing to the painting of Grandma in the straw hat, "but the frame is awful."

"It's too rustic," Libby agreed. "Looks like a cowboy framed it." She wrinkled her nose to show her disgust for cowboys generally.

"Dad did it," I said.

"It looks like a grocer did it, then," Libby said, and laughed. "With planks from orange crates."

"No, it looks more like he used those synthetic fireplace logs." Dan grinned.

"It is pretty grim-looking," I agreed. Dad had made the frame so that the portrait could be a gift from both of us. Grandma hadn't liked the portrait. I don't know how she liked the frame.

"Your dad is a cookie—I wasn't making fun of him," Libby said, seeing what I could only guess might be a sober look on my face. "It's a term of endearment," she explained to me. She looked up at Dan. "Russ really is a cookie," she said.

"A real chocolate chip off the old block." Then they both broke up laughing, something they often did late at night. The goofiest thing could set them off. It relieved the tensions of the day, I guess.

I smiled at them. "I think I'll go to bed now and think about having that painting reframed. I might just do that. I think I have gotten the point. Yesssireee." I danced a soft shoe out of the room, which kept them laughing.

But in my bed I felt sad. I hadn't liked the frame from the minute I saw it, but it was my dad's work, and it was his way of showing me that he was willing to enter my world of the arts a little bit, even though he didn't know a thing about it. It was done with loving intentions. But living around Libby and Dan forced me to see how wide the gap was between what my parents were and what I was and wanted to be. It made me really sad. And Libby and Dan snickering and guffawing in the kitchen, probably making more cookie jokes about my dad, didn't help either. I pulled the pillow over my head.

The first day of gallery hunting turned out to be a blazing success compared with what followed. Marian Laird had at least looked at my slides. She had at least invited me to come back when I had more work to show. In the two weeks that followed, twenty-three out of twenty-five galleries I visited told me that they were not interested in unsolicited work. One man called it "off-the-street art." "We just don't bother," he said. A woman said she was charmed by my naiveté. I could have kicked both of them in the knee.

Two people from different galleries did look at the slides briefly. One was a young woman at Mason's Gallery near Somerville. She said she really liked my stuff, but she only worked there and didn't have any authority to "take on new artists," and her boss, Mr. Mason, the owner of the gallery, was in Europe and wouldn't be back for a couple of months. She was so nice to me that I kind of hung around longer than I needed to and practically told her my whole life story. Trying to place paintings can really make a person act pathetic.

Then there was this older guy, Mr. Kruikshank, at Mystic Galleries Ltd., a really nice gallery on Church Street in Cambridge that he and his wife owned. He was eager to see my slides, almost gliding from behind his elegant cherry-wood desk to kiss my hand, his mustache grazing my skin. That kiss turned me into a toad, lumpy and speechless. I followed him into a back room, where he projected the slides onto a screen. "These are marvelous," he repeated over and over again. Occasionally he stroked my arm for emphasis. Toad that I was, I thought my lucky day had arrived. But his wife, Mrs. Kruikshank, appeared suddenly in the doorway. Her dyed black hair was pulled so tight to the back of her head that it slanted her eyes—I swear it. "I want to see you, Mr. Man," she said to Mr. Kruikshank. She actually called him that—Mr. Man—emphasizing the *m*'s. It was a command, not a request, and Mr. Kruikshank obeyed instantly. I could hear her beating him up verbally in loud whispers behind the wall. Only phrases of real words came through: "You have no right," and "I know your little game," "*my* money," "young nubile things."

I placed my slides back into the plastic containers and slipped quietly out of the gallery. I had visited twenty-five galleries in person and had gotten zip for it. Libby had told me to go in person because, she said, it was harder to reject a human being in the flesh.

Wrong. It was a cinch for all twenty-five. Being the rejected flesh wasn't so simple. I noticed in a plate-glass window that my shoulders were drooping along with my self-esteem. I decided to mail the slides from then on and concentrate my energies on new paintings. The reward I gave myself for all that gallery hunting was to eat lunch in Harvard Square and look for Willy. That, too, seemed like a futile activity now, but I wasn't ready to give it up yet. Whenever I could, I continued riding the subway into Cambridge. I continued to search the faces of the men moving along the sidewalk, hoping to be struck dumb at the sight of him.

When I got paid, I went to Swinton's, a frame shop off Harvard Square on Mt. Auburn Street, with Grandma's portrait. Sleigh bells hanging on the inside of the front door jingled when I entered the frame shop. A tall, angular woman, middle-aged, with long strawberry-blond hair tied back at her neck, greeted me. "Hi! Sorry for the mess," she said. "We're just finishing some remodeling."

Slats of timber leaned against the wall near a doorway leading to another room. The floor in the room where I was standing had traces of sawdust trampled into the carpet, and a film of dust covered the sample frames on the wall. A power saw turned on and off in the other room.

"Hi," I said, and set my painting down onto the counter. "I want to have this reframed."

"Good," she said. She flinched each time the power saw started up again. "And this is the painting you want framed?" she asked, suddenly focusing on Grandma's portrait.

"Yes," I said.

"This is nice," she said, standing the painting on end. "This is *very* nice. You are right to have it reframed," she said. "The frame is absolutely dreadful—doesn't do a thing for the painting. Do you have something in mind?"

The power saw started up again, and we both squinted at each other as if the noise affected our eyes. "Sorry," she said. "We had a tiny gallery out in the back room, which we've expanded, and we've got an open house next week and it has to be done." She rolled her eyes as if she didn't believe it could possibly be done by next week.

I nodded at her sympathetically.

"Eugene Stauffer is doing a slide show on the Roode family in Maine, and their son is going to be here to show some of his latest paintings." She emphasized the two names by lowering her voice and whispering them as if they were holy. I had no idea who they were. "Did you see his work in the *Boston Globe* a couple of months ago? He—Thomas—may be better than his father," she whispered as if conspiring. I could barely hear her above the whining of the power saw.

I tried to look impressed. "Walnut burl," I said.

She looked startled then. "What?" It came out almost like a hiccup.

"I'd like a highly polished walnut-burl frame—do you carry that?"

"Oh!" and she laughed. "Forgot where I was for a minute." She looked in back of her. "Well, we used to. It's hard to get sometimes." She rummaged through the shelves behind the counter.

"Hard to get" sounded expensive.

"Here's a piece. I'd probably have to order it." She laid it alongside the portrait, covering part of Daddy's handiwork. "That looks marvelous, doesn't it? I'm not sure I would have thought of it." She stood admiring it. "Who did this painting?"

"I did," I said.

"Really?" Her look had a new respect in it. "Do you have other paintings?"

"Yes." I hadn't thought of bringing my portfolio to a frame shop. "And I'm interested in selling them," I said quickly.

"Do you have slides?"

"Not with me, but I could bring some by tomorrow morning."

"I'd like to see them," she said. She measured the painting and pulled out a catalog to look up a price. "I like new artists—I'm Judy Swinton, by the way."

"I'm Susan Smith," I said. We shook hands.

"Oh, it's 'Susan'—I couldn't quite read your signature." She peered closely at it.

The silent 5 strikes again.

"I'll bring the slides tomorrow," I said quickly.

"Good," she said. She quoted me a price for the frame. It was almost one whole paycheck. "That's good," I said. "Starving artist" suddenly took on a new, personal meaning.

"It'll take at least a week—is that okay?"

"It's great. Thanks. Thanks a lot."

Outside on the sidewalk I felt like singing Italian arias. Somebody wanted to see my slides. Somebody liked "new" artists.

When I told Libby and Dan about Judy Swinton, they suggested I take Libby's car instead of the subway and take three or four paintings with me along with the slides. "If the paintings are right there in the shop, she might be more inclined to take them," Dan suggested.

"Take these." Libby pointed at the *Family Portrait*, the *Wheaties Portrait*, and a painting I had done of Derriere standing in the sandpile, the garden hose dangling from his hand like a common garden snake. He-Man and several G.I. Joes were half-buried in the sand.

"I don't know if I'll be able to find Harvard Square in the car—I always take the subway," I said.

"I'll draw you a map," Dan said. He drew on a paper towel.

"Parking will be the hardest part," Libby said.

"Tell me about it," I said. "I'll just run some little old lady down, yell at her for being in my way, and take her spot."

"That's the spirit," Libby said.

"You learn fast," Dan added.

The next morning I drove Libby's Toyota straight to Judy Swinton's frame shop. When an electrician's van pulled out of a parking spot directly in back of the shop, and I pulled into it, I knew it would be an extraordinary day. While Judy looked at the slides through one of those cheap plastic viewers you hold up to your eyes, I positioned the three paintings against the wall on the floor, which had even more sawdust plastered into the carpet than the day before, although the power saw was silent now.

Judy stood by me, still holding the slide viewer. She bent over to hold each painting away from the wall as she scrutinized it. She held the *Family Portrait* the longest. When she was finished, she stood back from them, pulled her braided hair around to the front, and held on to it with one hand.

I stood a little away from her with my fingers crossed behind my back, saying silent prayers to all the positive forces in the universe.

"Well, as long as you brought these, I'd like to hang them for the open house. I have more than enough space now," she said, brushing the braid across her lips. Did that mean that if I hadn't brought them, she wouldn't have wanted them? Did I care?

"I'll try to get the other portrait framed in time for the open house too," she said.

"Oh, thank you," I gushed. "Thank you. I'm so excited. This is just wonderful."

She smiled on me like a fairy godmother. "Come on, you need to fill out some forms, and I'll give you a flyer for the open house."

"I'll come, for sure," I said, "although I might be a little late—I work nights, but I can get off early, I think." If Salvatore wouldn't let me off work early, I'd quit.

"It's open house," she said. She had walked behind the counter. "Come whenever you can get here. People enjoy meeting promising young artists."

I was flattered that she thought of me as promising. I filled out the forms and left, floating out the door on little winglets like the cherubs in Tiepolo paintings. Resurrection day couldn't be a finer day than this one. I decided to push my luck, left the car in its parking place, and walked to Cardullo's in Harvard Square. I bought a ham sandwich and chocolate milk and took it out to the street plaza, where I sat on a bench and waited for Willy to walk by. I figure if the gods are with you in one thing, they're with you, period. You know, like those contestants on *The Price Is Right* who just can't lose. They come onstage, they win a car and $11,000 dollars on the wheel, and then they win the final showcase and come within $100 of the retail price and win both showcases. And it's usually their birthday too. You can see it on their faces: winners. That's the way I felt—like a winner. I was sure Willy would walk by my bench that day, and I would think of a way to bring him back into the family literally, the way I had painted him back into the family figuratively. I sat for an hour and a half in the sun. Willy didn't come.

At work Zella and I traded schedules for the day of the open house so that I worked the afternoon instead of the night shift.

At home I invited both Libby and Dan to go with me, and they said they wouldn't miss it for all the bisque in Boston. Then I called Fiona and told her every detail of my life. Then she told me every detail of her life, and before I knew it, we had talked an hour and a half.

✺ 5 ✺

Swinton's Frame Shop was already a party when Dan, Libby, and I arrived. Tubs of geraniums skirted the front of the store, together with a few round tables and chairs that hadn't been there a few days ago. Japanese lanterns were strung from the store to the streetlights, their light not making a bit of difference, since the sun hadn't gone down yet, and an accordion player stood out near the door playing "The Last Time I Saw Paris."

"The accordion player is overkill, I think," Libby said as we crossed the street plaza.

"I like it," I said.

The first room inside the frame shop was filled with people buying prints and drinking and eating from little plates. Judy Swinton was standing in front of the counter, which had been converted into a refreshment table. She was surrounded by people, answering questions, and when she saw me, she pointed into the new room, and said, "Slide show." She moved her mouth very deliberately so that I could read her lips in case I couldn't hear her. I nodded at Libby and Dan to follow me into the darkened room. There were a few single seats sprinkled among the last four or so rows, and we split up in favor of standing in the back. The narrator, who I guessed must be the critic, Eugene Stauffer, spoke in a

high musical voice with a lot of intensity and shifted his weight
from side to side, occasionally pointing at something on the screen,
his whole body falling into silhouette as his arm and hand became
the pointer. The slides showed mostly the Roode father's paintings
of New England landscapes and people, but sometimes a slide of a
sculpture would appear that belonged to the mother, Rosemary,
and he would apologize that we could not "know the energy of this
work" the way it ought to be known because we could only *sense* its
three dimensions in this two-dimensional slide show. I liked the
works I saw mostly, but Mr. Stauffer's voice soon irritated me.
There was a lot of B.S. about this guy. It wasn't that I didn't
believe what he said about the paintings, but the way he said it—in
this really affected voice—it was his tone I didn't like.

Finally he showed some of "young Thomas Roode's paintings." I
sat up with interest when I saw the first one. It was a floating
head. They were all floating heads. Big, fine, distinct, and individu-
alized heads, floating on the ocean like ships. It sounds strange,
and Mother and Grandma would certainly have detested them,
but I liked them immediately. They, too, were portraits. How had
the artist, "young Thomas," thought of it? It's all such a mystery.

When the slide show was over, Eugene Stauffer, whom I could
see now that the lights had been turned on, was a slight, angular
man with a paisley scarf tied loosely about his neck. He introduced
Thomas Roode. He was tall and wore baggy, navy-blue linen pants
and a white short-sleeved shirt with great-looking pockets and no
jacket. His sandy hair flopped down over one eye. He looked
slightly uncomfortable to have the smaller, older man fawning over
him in front of a crowd of people. He said he would be glad to
answer any questions about any of the works shown in the room.
We all clapped politely and stood up. I turned around to search for
Libby and Dan and saw in an instant my paintings on the back wall
—four of them. The rest of the room was filled with Roode-family
paintings, including a lot of floating heads, but one wall was mine
—Susan Smith's, silent 5 and all. I felt perfectly giddy.

"Did you see them?" Libby was at my shoulder. "They look marvelous." She nodded toward my paintings.

"The frame you chose for *The Woman in the Hat* is just right," Dan said. The surge of people around us pushed toward the door leading to the first room of the shop where the food was.

"Let's get something to drink and come back," Libby suggested.

I wanted to see the floating heads up close. "I want to see these paintings first," I said.

"We're dying of thirst, so we'll meet you in a few minutes— okay?" She and Dan were already halfway to the door.

I nodded and stepped back against the wall to get out of the way of the crush of people. A couple of guys were stacking the folding chairs away so that there would be more room to view the paintings. I waited against the wall until the room had cleared a little.

At the other end of the room two groups had gathered: one around Eugene Stauffer, who was enjoying the attention, his voice rising above the general clamor of the room, and the other one around Thomas Roode, who nodded shyly, almost smiling, when people greeted him. Often he shoved the hair that fell over his forehead back to the side of his head with a quick sweep of his right hand, only to have it fall right back down. He wasn't much older than I was, and I could tell he didn't like greeting strangers and had probably had to be talked into it. Who had done it? Judy Swinton? Eugene Stauffer? His parents?

When the chairs had all been removed, I made my way slowly along the wall where Thomas's floating heads hung. They were quite simply wonderful paintings, and I kept checking my own portraits at the end of the room to reassure myself that I really could paint. I now stood within hearing range of Thomas and two women who were gushing tributes to him. He muttered a modest thanks. I stood off to the side of them. They were the last of the group that had surrounded him, and when they left, he glanced at his watch.

"You are Thomas Roode," I said, as if he didn't know who he was, as if this were a true-false quiz.

He turned. "Yes."

"I'm Susan Smith," I said. "I painted the portraits down at the end of the room."

To my relief his face lit up and showed real interest. "Really? I wondered how you pronounced that five. I'm glad to meet you. Really glad."

We shook hands.

"Your portraits are just great," he continued. "I mean it. It's just really good painting." He smiled again eagerly and then bit his bottom lip as if to make himself stop.

"And I love these floating heads," I said. "I wish I'd painted them myself."

He stopped biting his lip and let the smile return. "Thanks," he said.

"Here you are!" Judy Swinton came out of nowhere and grabbed my arm. "You've met Thomas, I see."

"Yes," Thomas and I said in unison. He swept the hair off his forehead and grinned at me as if we had shared a joke.

"I want to introduce you to Gene. He is very interested in your *Family Portrait,*" she whispered, and nodded her head toward my painting, where Eugene Stauffer and his groupies were now gathered. He gestured at the different faces in the portrait with an elegant hand, interpreting, it seemed, my painting the way he had interpreted the Roode family's paintings. I was a little stunned. I watched him press his index finger across pursed, thoughtful lips. My painting seemed to have him perplexed. It made me smile and think of Picasso: why not try to understand the songs of birds?

Thomas, smirking slightly, leaned down to me. "Lucky you— you may be the subject of his next slide show," he said.

Judy held on to both of us and led us down to the other end of the room. Gene Stauffer looked older close up than he had from across the room. "Gene!" Judy interrupted him. "This is Susan

Smith from Springville, Utah, the artist of that painting. Susan, this is Gene Stauffer—oh, excuse me a minute," she said, responding to a call from the other room.

At first I thought "Gene" hadn't heard the introduction. "I thought it went very well, don't you, Tom," he said.

Thomas flinched slightly at being called Tom, and I made a mental note not to call him that. "It went just fine," he said.

"And you—my dear young butterfly—you have created a stir with these people." He pushed through some of them and pulled my arm snugly through his.

"I have?" I said. I wasn't sure I liked being called a young butterfly.

"Here's the artist herself, ladies and gentlemen," he said addressing the small group surrounding us as if they filled an auditorium. "Now we shall get it straight. You must tell us who all these people are in your painting."

I gave him the names as he pointed to them one by one. "That's an ancient Anasazi woman and her baby," I said when he pointed to her.

"Symbolic of?" His eyebrows arched into perfect points.

I didn't know the answer. I looked at Thomas, who towered behind Gene Stauffer's delicate frame. He shrugged his shoulders elaborately as if to say, "Beats me," which gave me courage to say, "I don't really know. I saw her in a museum in southern Utah several years ago."

Thomas smiled, but Gene Stauffer seemed disappointed. "Ahhh," he breathed. "But it seems to me there's an attempt here at"—his hand searched and circled the air—"a kind of necrophilic voyeurism." The group of people surrounding us looked from his face to mine.

"Is there?" I felt helpless. I really didn't have a clue what he was talking about.

Thomas was now grinning broadly over Stauffer's shoulder.

"What about this man here in the triangular shape? That certainly has sexual significance. The triangle has always been considered—"

"An artist should not have to explain her own painting," Thomas interrupted, grabbing my arm. "You should know that better than anyone, Gene," he chided, and pulled me away from the group.

"What was he talking about?" I asked him as we moved through the doorway into the main shop, where people were still eating and chatting. Accordion music wafted through the front door. It was now dark outside, and the lighted Japanese lanterns swayed gently from the wires.

"Who knows? Don't let him wrangle you into discussing it. He'll eat you up," Thomas said, handing me a drink. "My parents call him the smiling barracuda. Do they have any of those in Springville, Utah?" He handed me a cracker with sour cream and black beady-looking stuff piled onto it.

"We're too far inland for barracuda," I said. "We only have Mr. Mulford, who dresses up in his wife's clothes."

He guffawed. "Mr. Mulford?" he gasped.

I was pleased to make him laugh. "You know him?" I asked.

We stood grinning at each other.

"There you are." It was Libby. "We've met some friends of Dan's and we're sitting outside. So when you're ready, just come out. I didn't want you to think we'd gone without you or anything."

"Oh—" I said. "This is Thomas Roode. My aunt Libby."

"Libby Schroeder," she said. They shook hands. "Don't ever introduce me as your aunt again," she said to me playfully. "I'm not old enough." She told Thomas how much she liked his work, and Thomas thanked her. "See you in a while." She turned to leave. "Nice to meet you, Thomas." She walked outside.

"You live with your aunt?" Thomas asked me.

"Only for the summer."

"Then?"

"Then I'm supposed to go home and go to the university there,

but I'd really like to stay. I haven't told anyone that yet, though."
Except Fiona.

"Go to school here in Boston." He made it sound so simple.

"I'd like to, but—"

Three women stopped to talk to Thomas about his work and his
family, followed by a man and wife. I excused myself and went
over to thank Judy for hanging the paintings. "I'll come by to pay
for the frame tomorrow," I said.

"That's fine," she said. "I'd like to keep the paintings a little
while longer, if you don't mind."

"Great," I said.

Eugene Stauffer stood in the doorway and nodded at me, one
eyebrow arched. I nodded back. He just kept staring at me in this
ghoulish way, so I decided to go outside and join Dan and Libby
and their friends. It felt safer.

As I stepped across the threshold, Thomas's voice called from
behind me. "You're not leaving, are you?"

"Well—" Eugene Stauffer was still staring at me in this creepy
way.

"Wait just a minute." He turned and said a few more words to
the man and his wife and then walked outside with me. It was a
perfect summer night. Harvard Square was filled with people
dressed in cool cottons and khakis, lingering in front of shop windows and bookstalls. The accordion player had stopped playing
and was having a drink and talking to a woman with a silk shawl
thrown casually over one shoulder. Libby and Dan laughed with
another couple at a small table.

Thomas searched the tables for empty seats and then looked out
to the street plaza. "Let's go sit on a bench—I mean, do you have
time?"

I looked over at Libby and Dan. "I think so," I said. I signaled to
Libby where I was going, and she nodded back at me.

We sat in the plaza where I had sat many times before looking for Willy, and I found myself searching spontaneously for him now.

As if Thomas could read my mind, he asked, "Who is the guy in the triangle in your painting, anyway? Just curious." He smiled.

"Uncle Willy," I said, and I proceeded to tell him my whole life story. He listened attentively, quietly, resting his elbow on his knee and holding the hair away from his forehead. I gushed hopelessly, realizing as I talked nonstop that I had wanted to talk about Willy for years but hadn't been allowed to. Willy was *verboten* at home. I had frothed on about Willy to Fiona once, but she had said, "You sound like you're in love with this guy or something—yuck, in love with an uncle." The revulsion in her voice was unmistakable, so I was guarded about him with her. Thomas made it easy to talk. I even told him how Libby had thought she had seen him in Harvard Square twice. "I find myself looking for him," I said.

His eyes searched the street plaza as if he, too, was looking for Willy. "So this Willy really isn't your uncle. I mean, he's only your uncle through marriage," Thomas said. "He's not *family*."

"Not really. Not anymore."

"But he feels like family, so you painted him into the family portrait."

"Yes."

He leaned back against the bench and folded his arms. "You came to Boston to find him—Willy, I mean?"

"No!" I said. "I came to Boston so I could go through life high up on stilts and feel alive."

His eyes opened wide. "Excuse me?" he said.

I laughed. "No, really, I had this dream—" I babbled on. I enjoyed talking to him. I enjoyed it so much. The accordion music started up again. It woke me out of myself, and I suddenly felt embarrassed. "I've been doing all the talking," I said. "I don't know anything about you, except that you paint floating heads and come from a whole family of artists, which boggles my mind, by the way."

Thomas straightened himself as if he were starting a dissertation: "Born and raised in Boothbay Harbor, Maine. My parents still live there. My brother lives in Provincetown, on the Cape. I just finished my second year at Harvard, where I play backgammon when I'm not studying or painting, and"—he took a breath—"I'm just getting ready to leave for Italy to paint for the summer, thanks to a Fulbright scholarship."

My mouth dropped. I couldn't help it. "You're going to Italy for the summer?"

He nodded. "Rapallo. It's on the Mediterranean Sea. I can't be too far from water, or I dry up and die. I leave tomorrow night."

He had green eyes. That was the first time I noticed just how green his eyes were. "That's terrific," I managed to say, but it was followed with an involuntary sigh. In fact it was terribly disappointing. On some level I had already planned Thomas Roode into my summer, and now I found he wasn't even going to be remotely around. I almost wished I'd never met him at all.

An awkward silence grew between us. Both of us searched the square to see if something new was going on, but it looked the same as it had just minutes before.

We turned to each other at the same time: "When are you coming back?" I asked.

"When are you going home?" he asked. We spoke in unison and burst out laughing.

"You first," I said.

"I'll be back on the first of September. "Will you be here then?"

"My parents think I'm coming home at the end of August. I want to stay, but they'll want me to go to school, I mean—" I stopped and collected myself. "I'm not sure," I said.

"I choose to believe you'll still be in Boston in September."

"I choose to believe it too," I said.

It was a pact. We sat in a comfortable silence for several minutes. Across the plaza I saw Eugene Stauffer come out of the frame shop and walk up Mt. Auburn Street.

"What does 'necrophilic voyeurism' mean, anyway?" I asked Thomas.

He looked down at the cobbled street, his ears pink. "Well, I think it means you get your sexual kicks from looking at dead things." His head was bent so that his bangs covered his eyes.

"It does not!" I said.

"I think it does," he said, looking up and shoving his hair back with one hand. "I'm positive."

"You mean that Stauffer guy thinks that I—"

Thomas nodded. "At least that's what he was implying."

"That's obscene. You don't think that—"

"It's what he wants to think. That, and that triangles are sexually significant." He smiled.

"That's disgusting."

"Stauffer's a bit of a slime, but he does have a certain influence, so just be polite when you run into him. You know what he told me?"

"What?"

"He said floating heads are indicative of a castration complex."

"Oh, for heaven's sake!"

"In the eye of the beholder—" He nudged me gently.

Libby motioned me back to the table. "I have to go," I said, standing.

He stood too. "Well—" he said.

"Mmm."

"Well, I—" he said.

"Uhh."

He laughed. "We sound like a couple of floating heads," he said. "Your aunt's name is Libby Schroeder, and she's in the book?"

"Elizabeth Schroeder—she lives on Mt. Vernon Street." We walked toward Libby and Dan, who were standing now, waiting.

"In the fall, then . . ."

"In the fall, yes." We shook hands. "Have a good trip," I said.

"Thanks." He stuck his hands in his pockets and walked off

toward the door of the frame shop, stopped suddenly, and turned. "We'll paint the glass flowers at Harvard in September," he called back to me.

"I'd like that." I watched him disappear into the shop.

I turned to Libby and Dan. "What are the glass flowers?" I asked.

That night, lying in bed on my porch listening to the flying insects flit against the screened wall, I thought of the open house at Swinton's Frame Shop, glittering and sensuous. I had tasted champagne for the first time. Mother would have had a stroke, but needn't worry, because I thought it was very medicinal tasting. Nasty. So I drank cherry 7-Ups from a champagne glass. There is something about holding a champagne glass, the stem resting against the wrist, that made me feel urbane and civilized and beautiful all at once.

I thought of the slimy Gene Stauffer and his insinuating words and glances and felt a pang of revulsion. I thought of the Dutch painter, Vermeer, who wouldn't speak to art dealers and who didn't care about selling his paintings at all. I thought of Thomas's green eyes and Willy's blue ones. Where was he now?

And finally I wondered if there really was any sexual significance to the shape of the triangle.

I arrived home from work the following night to find Libby and Dan watching the eleven-o'clock news in the living room.

"You had a visitor," Libby said.

Dan reached for a framed picture lying on the table behind the sofa where they were seated. "He brought you this," he said, handing it over.

I dropped my handbag on the coffee table and took the picture, which was carefully double-matted under the glass. It was a watercolor from Thomas: a self-portrait. He had painted his own head floating on the ocean, and he had added one hand protruding from

the water to hold his bangs back from his forehead. A cartoonlike
bubble hovered above his head with the words, "See you in September!" printed on it. To the left of the head was a buoy with a
sign to Rapallo pointing one way and a sign to Boston pointing in
the opposite direction.

"Oh, it's wonderful," I breathed.

"Pretty fancy greeting card," Dan said. His mouth twitched
slightly as if he wanted to say more.

"He was sorry he missed you," Libby said. "He was on his way to
the airport and couldn't stay."

"But he wanted to be *sure*"—Dan took an exaggerated tone—"to
be *very sure* that you saw his address in Italy on the back."

Libby elbowed him gently.

I turned the watercolor over. Thomas's careful printing deco-
rated one corner. I ran my finger across it. "It must have taken him
all day to do this," I said, turning the picture over again.

"You can be sure of it," Dan said.

"It's nice, isn't it?" I said, looking up. I clasped the painting to
my chest.

"*He's* nice," Libby corrected. "He's very nice."

"I don't understand," my mother said to me over the phone the
next morning. "Your paintings are hanging in a frame shop?"

"Well, it's more than a frame shop," I explained. "It started out
as a frame shop, but Judy, the woman who owns the shop, has
expanded it gradually so that now it's also a gallery, and she had
kind of a grand opening last night. She had a whole room full of
paintings by this family called Roode—their son was there—anyway, I've had my first showing in Boston."

"I thought you said it was in Cambridge."

"It's the greater Boston area," I said.

"Well, it's nice, Susan. Really, I think it's wonderful. This will be
a summer you'll always remember." She was into her mother
mode. "I've always been glad that I spent that summer before I got

married down in Tucson working for the scientists at the observatory there. I had so much fun." She paused briefly. "Even if you don't sell anything this summer, it will have been worth it—the *experience* will have been worthwhile."

She made it all sound so temporary. I felt a cold wind at my back standing there in Libby's hot and humid kitchen. "I am enjoying myself," I said, but I wanted to get off the phone. I didn't want to talk about going home. I hadn't been away that long yet.

"I've got some mail from the university for you. It may be your registration information."

"I've already registered," I said.

"Oh, well then, I'll just send whatever it is to you. By the way, I ran into Mr. Tuttle the other morning at the store, and he said there was a real shortage of art teachers in secondary schools right now, and he said that if you were interested in teaching, you were starting out at a really good time."

Thanks a bunch, Mr. Tuttle. "I don't want to teach art, Mom. I want to be an artist."

"It's always good to have a backup," she said. "I'll send you the stuff from the U."

"Thanks, Mom." I wondered if my voice sounded as strained as it felt.

"I love you."

"I love you too."

∽ 6 ∽

The idea of Grace McGregor's apartment, stuffed to the ceilings with her forty years of accumulated junk, fascinated me. It was the "narrow paths" cut through the stacks of magazines and old newspapers that especially fired my imagination. I thought of Grace as living in a self-imposed maze, lit by a single, bare, bright bulb at the center. I sketched her in dark, narrow tunnels, with walls of stacked empty dog food cans or empty chocolate-raisin cartons. I wanted to see the inside of her apartment more than anything I could think of.

To accomplish this, I bought chocolate raisins at the Bijou to give to Grace and Priceless. I figured that it would give me an excuse to knock on Grace's door and maybe get at least a peek at what was inside. But when I reached the top of the stairs, she was already out in the hall, the precious Priceless luxuriously cushioned in the crook of her arm.

"I suppose they don't teach recitation in the public schools anymore?" It was a rhetorical question; she barely stopped for air. "A shameful shortsightedness, if you ask me," she said. "I was the best in my class when it came to recitation." She pronounced *recitation* with the same reverent tone of voice that some people say *Nobel prize.*

"Have you heard 'Elegy Written in a Country Churchyard'? Now *that's* a great poem." She heaved up her breasts. " 'Elegy Written in a Country Churchyard,' by Thomas Gray." It was an announcement.

I pulled my key out of my bag.

" 'The curfew tolls the knell of parting day, The lowing herd . . .' " Her voice grew louder, and the vibrato intensified into a warble. Priceless stared at her patiently. *I* stared at her patiently, now standing in the open doorway of Libby's apartment waiting for her to finish. It seemed like the poem lasted an hour and a half. She bowed when she was done.

I clapped, because it seemed to be expected. "That's very impressive," I said.

She leaned into me with the dog and in a lowered voice asked, "Can you recite any poems by William Shakespeare?"

I shook my head.

" 'When icicles hang by the wall and Dick the shepherd blows his nail—' "

"I'll have to hear that one later," I interrupted. "I'm just getting home from work, and I'm starving."

"I haven't eaten either," she said, looking past me into the apartment.

"We could eat together," I said, "at *your* place. I have some potato salad and some other stuff I'll bring over . . ."

She looked at me hard. "Never mind," she said. "I've got some things to do." She turned away to her apartment.

I shut the door and felt a little slimy for trying to trap her. But not so slimy that I was going to quit trying.

I slapped potato salad between two pieces of white bread: a potato salad sandwich. Washing it down with milk, I gulped it as fast as I could and then pressed my ear to the front door. Not a sound. I pulled the chocolate-covered raisins from my bag and went back out into the hall. It was empty. I stood in front of Grace's door and knocked as boldly as I could: a loud, authoritative knock. It sent a rush of blood to my head. I stood directly by the opening of the door so that even if she opened it only a crack, I'd be able to see something. Anything.

"Who is it?" Grace's muffled voice called from behind the door.

"Susan—I forgot to give you something."

There was a shuffling behind the door, and then the doorknob turned. Grace squeezed her hefty body through the narrowest possible opening of the door. I tried to look behind her, but there was nothing but blackness. Not even a single light bulb. Did she live in the dark?

She pulled the door shut behind her. "What is it?" she asked.

"It's not much," I began apologizing. "Just some chocolate-covered raisins from the theater where I work. I know you and Priceless like them." I handed the box to her.

She turned them over in her hands. "You didn't have to do that," she said.

"I—I know that. It's just that I—I—" I stammered. "They sit in the case, rows of them, and they remind me of you, and so I decided to buy one for you. I mean, it's really nothing." I was embarrassed for all kinds of reasons.

She looked down at the box of raisins in her hand. "Thank you." She sighed. "Libby told me you were a portrait painter," she continued.

"Yes."

"She said you were very good," she said.

"I'm still learning," I said.

"I have something to show you." She unlocked the door.

Again I tried to see beyond the door through the narrow opening she allowed for herself, but I couldn't see anything. She was gone only a few minutes and returned with a brown photograph of a man in a military uniform in a tarnished silver frame. I could hear Priceless scratching on the other side of the locked door.

Grace kicked the door lightly. "Quiet, bad dog," she said. She wiped the dust off the portrait. "Nice-looking, isn't he?" she said, holding out the picture.

"Yes, he is," I said. "Is he your husband?"

"Lord, no." She gave me an exasperated look as if I had rutabaga for brains. "He's my son, Sean." She said it softly, with great affection.

"I didn't know you had a son," I said.

"He's dead. He died in World War Two. He was a bomber pilot."

I thought of Willy.

"He was such a good boy," she said. "He was always a good boy." She sighed.

I didn't know what to say.

"He's been dead for forty years, and I still miss him terribly. He was such a joy of a child. If I had it to do over again, I wouldn't let him go." Her voice grew fierce. "I'd take him to Switzerland or somewhere, but I wouldn't let the military take him. I wouldn't let him die. They could pull my hair and fingernails out, I wouldn't let him die again. I've had over forty years to think about it, and I know what I'm saying."

This side of Grace, so gentle and fierce, without theatrics, made me speechless.

"I want you to have it," she said, pushing the framed photograph into my hands.

"I couldn't possibly," I said, pushing it back at her. "It's too little to have of him as it is."

"You could paint him," she said. "You could paint his portrait." She had let go of the frame, so that I was left holding it. "It wouldn't take too long, would it?"

I smiled warily at her. I had begun the evening thinking I could outfox Grace McGregor into showing me her apartment, and now she had outfoxed me into painting a portrait of her long-dead son.

"It won't take long," I said.

By the time Libby got home, I had already made several

sketches of Sean McGregor's face. They weren't very interesting, drawn from a photograph. What I really wanted to work on was a painting of Grace standing out by the stairwell holding Priceless as she always did, only the dog's head would be replaced with her son's head. But since this was a commissioned piece, so to speak, I decided to do it straight for once. But it was like painting by the numbers. I felt like a fraud, a painter of propaganda. I exaggerated his beauty and painted a vision.

∼ 7 ∼

I borrowed Libby's car to collect my paintings from Judy Swinton, who was sorry none of them had sold—although, she hastened to add, there had been a lot of interest in them and asked if I would come by in a few months to show her my new stuff. I said I would.

After I locked the paintings into the car, I stopped to buy a sack lunch at Cardullo's. I sat on a vacant bench in the shaded street plaza where I had sat with Thomas the night of the open house. I ate the sandwich, watching the people in their pastel and white summer clothes drift along the sidewalks, and I wished I had some watercolors and paper to paint them with. The sun was hot and made me feel dreamy, even though I was wide awake. So dreamy, I thought I saw Uncle Willy in white shirt and pants, standing over a display of books outside a shop just below Church Street. His tall, lean body was tanned, and he wore sandals on his feet. His black hair was longer than Willy's military cut. He bent over a book, slowly leafing through the pages. In my dream state I believed he was Willy. What would I say to him?

Uncle Willy, it's me, Susan, Marianne's niece.

He would look at me blankly perhaps.

You used to swing me by my ankles and wrists around the backyard in Springville, Utah, about ten years ago. You called it flying. Do you remember? I gave you a picture wrapped in curled ribbon and you said you would hang it above your bed. I never saw you again, but you sent me this silver armadillo necklace on my eighth birthday, and I've worn it ever since.

I watched the man pay for the book and glance at his watch.

Willy, you understood the importance of the changing light, the smell of the paint. I have loved you all my life.

He turned his head and looked down the street in my direction. I started. *Willy?* I rubbed my eyes. The sun was so hot. It could disorient a person, but I could see his face plainly now. He took sunglasses from his shirt pocket and put them on. Willy—it *was* Willy—walked toward me, his head bowed over the book.

I collected the rest of my lunch in the paper sack and folded the edges carefully, tightly, keeping my eyes on Willy. I sat, paralyzed, with the sack and my canvas bag gathered in my lap.

Willy crossed into the street plaza, looked casually over the benches, which were now mostly occupied, and sat down next to me. The coincidence of seeing Willy at all, let alone having him walk right to my bench, was so staggering that all I could do was swallow several times in succession. At the same time—and this is so weird—I was aware of the pleasing composition we must make, both of us dressed in summer white, only partially shaded under the maple tree. I felt like I was sitting inside my own painting, silent, unable to speak.

Willy sat reading a book called *How to Pyramid Small Business Ventures.* Suddenly he closed the book, laid it in his lap, and stretched his arms so that his elbows were resting on the back of the bench. He was almost touching me, and I could smell him. I felt seven years old again. And still I couldn't speak. It was as if my mother and Marianne and Libby, too, were sitting on my shoulder telling me not to—whispering about the china and the Francis I sterling silver, about abandonment, and the FBI and sociopaths. That's what I had heard Mother call Willy—a sociopath. I looked it up. It meant "a person who is hostile to society." That didn't describe Willy at all. I remembered when he taught me to polka in the kitchen right after he and Marianne were married. Marianne and Mother and Dad were laughing their heads off because I was so little and looked so awkward, and Willy was yelling above the laughter and above the "Beer Barrel Polka" playing on the stereo, "Raise those knees, girl! Raise those knees!" I couldn't have been more than five years old. Where was the hostility? I didn't get it.

Was Willy a *dangerous* person? No one who smelled that good could be dangerous. And I wasn't seven anymore; I was seventeen. I could take care of myself. "Hello, Willy," I said softly.

Willy jerked forward at the sound of his name and glanced nervously at the others sitting on the benches and then at me. "Do I know you?" he asked. His hand moved up to adjust his sunglasses.

"I'm Susan," I said. "Susan Smith—Russ and JoAnne's daughter."

"Marianne's niece," he said slowly. I wondered if that was the first time he had said Marianne's name in ten years.

"Yes."

He looked me over, "Girl, you sure have changed. You've grown up." He said this with a kind of appreciation that made me glad I was grown up.

"Yes," I said. "I have." I laughed nervously.

"Little Susan."

I laughed again.

"I used to swing you around your backyard by your hands and your feet. Do you remember?"

I nodded. "I loved it when you did that," I said. My neck felt extra hot, and I looked down at my sandals and swallowed.

"So what are you doing here in Cambridge?"

"Actually I'm living in Boston for the summer—with Libby— Aunt Libby."

His back straightened immediately, and his eyes darted among the three benches.

"She's not here. She works. I'm alone," I reassured him.

"It's not that I wouldn't like to see Libby," he said quickly. "But—"

"It's that you don't want to be found," I said.

"Exactly," he said. His body relaxed a little, and he leaned back into the bench.

"*They* used to come asking for you at the house," I said.

"They? Oh, *they!*" He grinned. "I'll bet your mother didn't like that." He seemed to be looking off into the distance. "Your mother didn't especially care for me, I don't think."

"I don't know about before you left, but she hasn't liked you a whole lot since you left." I smiled at him. I didn't want him to think that I felt the same way as my mother. He returned the smile. He was even better-looking than I remembered.

We both looked down. "Well," we said at the same time, and laughed again. I think I said "Gee whiz," like a dumb goose.

"And Marianne? How's Marianne doing?" He laid his arm across the back of the bench. I could feel it when I sat back.

"She just got married. Just a few weeks ago—to Heber McIntyre. She lived in an apartment in our basement and had a beauty salon for the last ten years. Heber's an industrial fisherman off the coast of Alaska. He's my mother's age. They grew up together." I watched Willy's face for any sign of pain or loss, but I didn't see any. He had one leg crossed over his knee, and he was playing with the strap of his sandal.

"Ten years, huh?" He seemed to be calculating. "You must be about eighteen now." He looked up.

"I will be in August," I said. "I just graduated from high school. I have an art scholarship to the university, but I don't know—"

He nudged me with his arm. "Girl, you restless like your uncle Willy?"

"Maybe," I laughed. "I'm a portrait painter and I've won some prizes. I'm thinking of taking a year out to paint."

"A painter, huh. Do you need an agent?" he asked. "I could be your agent."

I laughed at him. He was so eager. "Well, maybe," I said. I told him about my job at the Bijou.

"Do you get any free passes?" he asked. He was standing up. He was getting ready to leave.

"Sure. Come by anytime, and I'll get you in," I said. I didn't know anything about the free passes, but I wanted to see him again. I told him the nights I worked. "Please come," I begged him. I lowered my voice. "I won't tell Libby I saw you. I won't tell anyone," I whispered. "And it will be free."

"Girl, that's the magic word." He looked off down the street. "I've gotta go," he said quickly. "You sure have grown pretty as a picture." He walked off up the street toward Massachusetts Avenue.

"Don't forget," I called. "It's the Bijou on Washington Avenue."

He waved his arm at me. Other women watched him as he walked down the street. I wanted desperately to follow him, to find out where he worked, where he lived. I didn't want to lose sight of him. And I did take a few steps forward—then stopped. The thought that Willy was a slippery kind of guy came to me, uninvited, and I wondered if I would ever see him again. *Slippery* was the exact word that came to mind. But then, *slippery guy* could have been my mother's voice and not my own. Sometimes it's hard to tell them apart. Holding the silver armadillo between my fingers, I made a wish.

I wrote Thomas about meeting Willy in Harvard Square. "It's like he walked right out of the triangle," I wrote him. I told him of the full-length portrait I had started of Willy, which I kept hidden under my bed, and I sent him sketches of him: Willy, his hands in his pockets, his beautiful face and eyes, his dark hair, his smiling mouth.

At night, sitting with Libby on her bed, both of us in pajamas, I wanted desperately to talk about Willy. I really wanted to tell her that he lived here and that I saw him and talked to him. I wanted to tell her how handsome he was.

"Did Willy gamble?" I asked. It seemed like a safe enough question.

"Your mother seemed to think so."

"She hates Willy."

"Now—but I don't think she hated him at first. He was very charming, you know. Everyone liked him."

"You too?"

"Heavens, yes. I mean, what was there not to like? He was handsome and spoke in that charming, soft Texan drawl of his. He always bought little presents for everyone—probably with Marianne's money—and he was full of compliments: 'Girl, you sure can dance. I'll bet you and me could win one of those dancing contests!' " She mimicked Willy perfectly and laughed at herself.

"I thought he was wonderful," I said. *I think he's* still *wonderful,* I thought to myself.

"He was good with kids," she said. "In the end he was nothing but a taker. He never gave anything of value."

My hand automatically sought the armadillo necklace. Mother had always said it was an *expensive* necklace made of *real* silver.

Libby understood the gesture and reached over to cover my hand with her own. "I don't mean that the necklace he gave you isn't valuable. I mean that he never gave of himself. You couldn't rely on Willy to be there when you really needed him. He really hurt Marianne by leaving the way he did. She was devastated."

"I know," I said, bored. "He took the Royal Doulton china and the Francis I sterling silver." I said it in a singsongy voice, trying to imitate my mother.

Libby didn't smile. "No," she said gravely. "That isn't what hurt. He abandoned her, Sue. He *abandoned* her. Whatever problems they had, he wasn't willing to talk or negotiate or compromise. He left. He abandoned her," she repeated.

"Oh," I said.

It was time to change the subject. "Couldn't we invite old Grace over one of these days? You know, for dinner or something?" I asked Libby. I had decided that if Mrs. Whitten could get into Grace McGregor's apartment, so could I, but first I had to get her to trust me. The invitation had to come from her. I wouldn't be able to bully her into it. I'd tried, and it hadn't worked.

Libby grimaced. "She drives me nuts. She dried up any milk of human kindness coursing through my veins. Sometimes I think that if I see another 'Priceless' dog trick, or hear Gray's 'Elegy' one more time, I will start into a lifetime of projectile vomiting."

"You have a real way with words," I said. "Do you mind if I invite her to *lunch*? She'll be gone by the time you get home. I feel sorry for her."

"Why?"

I thought a moment. "I'm like her," I said.

"What?"

"I'm like her. There's something inside of me that is like her. I don't know exactly what it is. I'm a little afraid of it. It's something about me that's pathetic. That's the way it feels, at least, like something pathetic that I share with her."

"*She's* pathetic. You're not."

"I just hide it better."

"*Everybody's* pathetic in some way."

I couldn't explain it any differently, or maybe I just didn't want to. It was a kind of neediness. For Grace it was a need to be loved by anyone at all. For me it was a need to be loved by someone other than those who already loved me. Or to be loved more completely. It's so hard to explain, because it's embarrassing to feel so hard up. But inside I often felt as if I, too, were standing in a hallway, waiting for passersby to notice me and love me as I was, even if I had zits on my soul. Insisting on the silent 5 in my name was related to all of it somehow.

$\backsim 8 \backsim$

Libby said it was fine with her if I wanted to invite Crock and Canine over for lunch. Needless to say, Grace accepted the invitation. She came right on time. In fact I had the feeling that she stood outside the apartment door watching her wristwatch, and when the second hand showed a precise twelve o'clock noon, she rapped on the door.

"You're right on time," I said, letting her in.

"Say 'hi' to Susan, Priceless," she said, walking in. She made Priceless's paw wave to me.

"Hi, Priceless," I said. The two of them followed me into the kitchen.

"Oh, you have carnations!" Grace gushed. "Did you buy them just for this lunch? I hope you didn't get them just because I was coming."

"Why not?" I asked. I pulled a chair out for her.

"That's so nice. Smell, Priceless." She shoved the dog's head into the centerpiece. "He likes them," she said.

Priceless looked doggy dumb to me. "I hope you like clam chowder," I said, setting the steaming tureen on the table.

"Oh, I do," she cooed. "We both do, don't we, Priceless?"

I wondered if I should have set a place for Priceless.

"He can share with me," Grace said, answering my silent question. Her eyes glittered with excitement. It made me really glad I had invited her.

"You know," she said, "I haven't been in this apartment for over a year." She fingered the linen napkin as if she was guessing its value and finally dropped it into her lap.

I spooned soup into her bowl, then mine, and sat down.

Grace tasted the chowder. "This"—she pointed at the soup—"is good—really good." She encouraged Priceless to slurp from her spoon, which he did freely. "Priceless likes it too," she said. "Libby and Dan Lavenstein—you know, *downstairs*"—she took on a confidential tone, leaned forward across the table, and lowered her voice to a whisper—"they're an *item,* you know." She placed a finger across her lips. "Shhh," she said. "They don't want anyone to know."

"But *you* know." I smiled to think of it.

"Everyone in the building knows—probably all of Massachusetts knows, but if they want it to be a secret, we'll let them have it, won't we?"

I laughed. "I guess so," I said. I watched her blow on her soup.

"How is the painting of Sean coming?" she asked me.

"I've only done the preliminary drawings. Would you like to see them?" I stood up without waiting for her answer and got my notebook from the back porch. I could hear her slurping her soup.

I opened the notebook for her to see.

Grace caressed the page with her fingertips. "That's him—oh my." There were tears in her voice.

"You need to tell me the color of his eyes, his hair, his skin."

"His hair was golden," she began. "His eyes were the color of the sky early in the morning, when you're not sure whether it's going to be cloudy or sunny."

"Gray?"

"With yellow and green specks. His skin was smooth and soft.

He never had acne problems, like some children. Red cheeks—he had good color."

Inwardly I sighed. She made him sound like a god.

"I'll do the best I can," I said, closing the notebook.

She looked at me quizzically—the same look Priceless often had. "Do you want to see Priceless eat from a spoon?" she asked. It was trick time.

"Sure."

She pulled some chocolate-covered raisins out of her dress pocket and laid them in her soup spoon. "Dinner!" she yelled at Priceless. "Dinnertime!" Priceless covered the spoon with his black lips and gulped down the raisins.

"Now, if you could just teach him not to click the spoon," I said.

Grace looked at me hard. "What?"

"Just kidding," I said. "It was a joke."

She placed more raisins onto the spoon, and Priceless repeated the trick. He really was pretty amazing. First, because he ate chocolate-covered raisins at all, and second, because he ate them from a spoon. He was better than any dog I'd ever seen on the *David Letterman* show on his "Stupid Pet Tricks" segments.

"You should put Priceless on TV," I said. "No, really!" I said, arguing against the skeptical look on her face. "Haven't you seen the *David Letterman* show? Priceless is better than any of the dogs I've seen on there. Really!"

"I daresay he is," Grace said. "I daresay he is."

"I know how we could get you on there," I said. The idea was growing. "I'll make a video of you and Priceless doing all his tricks. You can explain them as you go, and then we'll send the video along with a carefully composed letter to the *David Letterman* show and wait for a reply. It'll work. I bet it will. You'd be on national TV. You'd be famous!"

I could see she liked the idea. "I wonder," she began, "if they might like me to recite some poetry too. Recitation is one of my fortes, you know. Have you heard 'Elegy Written in a Country Churchyard'?"

"Recite it for me while I clear up the dishes and get our dessert," I said.

She began, her voice taking on a dramatic tone that quickly crossed over the border into overacting. She gestured with her free arm and even looked heavenward, eyes rolling. I decided the poetry reading should end the video. David Letterman would love it.

I served chocolate cake for dessert. Priceless had a piece on his own plate and was the first to finish. He did not eat with a fork. After cake I called Libby at work to make sure it was all right if I used her video camera.

"Of course," she said. "Are you going to photograph Boston?"

I told her my plan. "That should be something," she said.

"I'm counting on it," I said.

I moved the table out of the middle of the kitchen, and that's where I recorded Priceless jumping through Grace's arms, through the quilting hoop, jumping for chocolate-covered raisins, eating them from a spoon, dancing on his hind legs and singing, all with Grace rewarding him with wet kisses and exclaiming into the video camera in a loud voice, "He's an old dog, you know—same age as me—eighty-four. That's twelve in dog years and eighty-four in people years. Imagine *me* jumping through hoops at my age!" I had the camera focused right on her face when she talked. She ended by reciting the "Elegy," sweeping her baggy arm in a large gesture for the lines "Can Honor's voice provoke the silent dust, Or Flattery soothe the dull cold ear of Death?"

When we were finished, we watched the video on Libby's television. "There you are, Priceless. That's you!" Grace said excitedly.

The dog sang along with itself on the video.

"I should have put on more lipstick," Grace said during the first close-up.

I sent her home with the rest of the chocolate cake. "Libby and I will work on a letter," I said. I followed her to her door. She stood with her back against it.

"Thanks for the beautiful lunch," she said. "Priceless loved it too."

"Maybe we could do it again."

"I'd like that."

"At your place," I said. "I'd like to see your place."

"No."

"I really would."

"No. It's not nice-looking like Libby's."

"I don't care about nice-looking."

"No."

"Well—g'bye, then. I'll send the video to the *David Letterman* show."

"Good-bye, and thank you for a wonderful afternoon." She didn't unlock her apartment door until I was safely inside Libby's apartment. It made me more curious than ever.

Libby was delighted with my video and laughed all the way through it. "The camera angles are hilarious," she said. "I should have hired you to work for me this summer." She composed a letter to David Letterman, written as if it were from Grace herself, requesting to be on the "Stupid Pet Tricks" segment of the show.

"Let's have Grace sign it," she said when we had typed up a finished copy.

"No," I said. "She doesn't know it's called 'Stupid Pet Tricks.' "

"Aha," she said, and signed it herself.

We stuck the letter in a book bag along with the videotape and addressed it all to David Letterman in New York.

Thomas sent me a letter saying he was into Mediterranean fish these days. "Don't tell the Fulbright people, and I won't tell your aunt about your seeing the notorious Uncle Willy. Have you seen him again?" In the margin of the letter he had drawn several species of fish with black ink and colored them in with pastels.

The names of the fish were beautifully printed under each picture. I laid the thin sheets of paper side by side on my desk. They were lovely enough to frame. I pinned a couple of the sheets to the wall above the desk next to the watercolor he had given me. I kept the sheet with Willy's name on it and stuck it in a drawer.

I looked through my drawings and decided to send him some of Grace and Priceless. I also sent him some pressed forget-me-nots that I was saving in my dictionary. "Found these growing out of a sidewalk on Pinckney Street," I wrote him. "Feed them to your Mediterranean fish."

∞ 9 ∞

Tuesday night was "dollar night" at the Bijou, and there was always a horrendous crowd that showed up, so that often Salvatore sold tickets and made Sweeney help Zella and me in the concession stand. I don't know how I had the time to look up between handing out jujubes and chocolate-covered raisins and making change, but when I did, I saw him—Willy—talking to Salvatore in the ticket booth. Salvatore was shaking his head at Willy and gesturing for him to move out of the line, which was halfway down the block. Willy wasn't moving. I made change for this girl for a Coke and large popcorn and heard my name shouted across the lobby: "Susan Smith, get over here, please." It was Salvatore. I could tell he was mad. I pushed my way through the crowd of people gathered in the lobby until I stood next to Willy. "Hi, Willy," I said.

"You know this guy?" Salvatore asked me.

"Yes, he's an old friend from Utah," I said.

"That explains it," Salvatore said sourly. "He says you told him you could get him a pass?"

"I did." I turned to Willy. "I'm sorry, I forgot to have it ready for you. I wasn't sure you'd come."

"Look, Sue, there ain't no such thing as a—"

"Just pass him through now, Mr. Zaccardi. I'll take care of it later. Thank you very much." I held my breath and hoped that Salvatore would cooperate.

Salvatore stared at me briefly and then handed Willy a ticket. "Have a nice evening," he said sarcastically.

"I will," Willy said.

"I'm so glad you came," I said in a rush. "I wasn't sure you would." I was following him through the crowd in the lobby. He was all dressed in white again, which made his face appear even more swarthy.

"That guy's got a rod up his—"

"Oh, that was my fault. Salvatore is really a good guy. I just hadn't explained it to him. Really, I'm sorry about it."

The crowd pushed us together face-to-face. "It's all right, girl." I could feel his soothing breath on me. "It really is all right." He smiled so warmly, I thought I'd died and gone to heaven.

Seriously. You know those stories about people who have died for a short time and have been revived? They all say they've seen Jesus and he's brighter than any light we can comprehend, and he makes them feel loved like they've never been loved before. He makes them feel all warm and fuzzy. That's how Willy made me feel.

"Come in and watch the movie with me," Willy said. We were still pressed in nose-to-nose.

"I can't now," I said. "I can join you the second hour. I'll bring some popcorn and drinks."

"I'll save you a seat."

"Susan Smith, do you still work here?" Salvatore's voice thundered across the lobby.

"Gotta go," I said quickly, and squeezed through the crowd to the concession stand, my face burning hot. I worked busily for twenty minutes until the movie began. I never looked up, but I was sure Salvatore was checking me out from wherever he was posted in the lobby.

"What do you mean telling him we have movie passes?" he asked later, leaning over the glass counter. "You know better than that!"

I pulled a dollar bill out of my pocket. "I know," I said, handing him the money. "It's just that I was afraid I wouldn't see him again, so I had to make something up. It was the only thing I could think of."

"You mean you had to pay him to get him to come to see you?" His long, oily hair fell over his forehead.

"No!"

"He needs a pass for a movie that costs one lousy buck? Who is he anyway?" His lips formed a snarl.

"He used to be married to my aunt a long time ago, and he was really good to me. I haven't seen him in ten years." I decided to say nothing about his deserting the air force. "He was so wonderful."

Salvatore's eyes narrowed in cynicism. "The guy is a slime," he said in a low voice so that Zella, who was making more popcorn, couldn't hear him.

"You don't know him," I said.

"Some people use a gun to get what they want. He uses his face." He turned and walked toward his office.

"That's not true," I called after him. "I'll be back in a minute," I said to Zella, and left the concession stand.

"That's not true," I said again, facing Salvatore in his crummy office. "You don't know anything about him, and you shouldn't be saying that kind of thing."

"I know about him."

"What do you mean you KNOW? You don't KNOW anything. You just met him."

"I KNOW guys like him." He sat on the top of his desk, his arms folded in front of him. His face looked so arrogant, I wanted to punch him with my fist. I wanted to see him bleed.

"You don't know anything, and I don't care what you think," I said.

He shrugged.

We both stared at each other in stubborn silence. I had never done anything with Salvatore except laugh and make jokes, and I wondered if we'd be able to get back to that. I didn't know if it was worth working there if I couldn't joke around with him. He was ruining everything.

"I should have told you, I guess." It was as close as I could come to an apology.

He shrugged again. "I may have overreacted to the guy's face," he said.

Another silence.

I swallowed. "I need a favor—you won't like it, but I really need it," I said. I sounded so dumb and desperate. "I need you to make some kind of theater pass for Willy."

He didn't say anything.

"I'll pay for every movie he comes to, but I don't want him to know. It won't cost *you* anything. You could make it on Bijou stationery or something and sign your name. I can put it in one of those little plastic containers, you know, and make it all look real official and everything." I was talking way too fast.

"Look, Sue—"

"Please, Salvatore. I beg you. Please. It's such a little thing."

"I don't feel so good about this," he said. He had moved around his desk and was taking stationery out of a drawer, which meant he was going to do it. I felt so relieved.

He typed out a note, signed it, and gave it to me for Willy. "I don't feel good about it," he said again.

When I was finished with my work, I bought popcorn and a Coke and went in to watch the rest of the movie with Willy, who sat on the aisle near the back of the theater. He had saved me a seat.

"Thanks, girl," he whispered when I handed him the popcorn. "I'm afraid I got you into trouble tonight. I'm sorry."

"No. No, you didn't—really. Here." I handed him the phony

pass that Salvatore had made up. "You can come anytime now, and they'll just let you through. Every employee is allowed one pass for a guest. Really."

"That's very nice of you." We were face-to-face. He was smiling at me. "Your hair still glows in the dark," he said.

I tried to cover my hair with my hands. "Don't say that," I said.

"Why not? I got it from your mother. She used to say she loved to look at you while you were sleeping in your crib, because your hair glowed in the dark like a halo. She said you brought sunshine into the house."

"Mother said that?"

"Yes, and she was right. I'm surprised they haven't outlawed you inside the theater." He laughed when I made a face.

Someone shushed us from behind. "Go home and watch TV if you wanna talk."

"Up yours," Willy said under his breath. We both snorted these stifled laughs, but we stopped talking.

I sat, enjoying Willy's presence. He made me believe in the string theory of the universe—how we're all connected by these vibrating strings and how everything we do affects everything else around us. I was enjoying Willy's vibrations.

After the movie Willy walked me around the Boston Common up toward Beacon Hill. "How's your painting coming?" he asked.

"Fine. Four of them are being shown in Swinton's Frame Shop in Harvard Square."

He thought a moment. "Oh, yeah—where Mt. Auburn curves."

"Yes. She put a price tag of twelve hundred dollars on one of them. Can you believe it?"

Willy blew softly through his lips. "Girl, you must be good," he said. "My girl must be mighty talented."

I liked it when he called me his girl. I liked it a lot. I hoped he would say something about the painting I did for him before he left ten years ago. I wanted him to say that he had pasted it above his bed like he said he would do, but he didn't say anything about it. I told him about Thomas Roode's floating heads and made him laugh.

"Well, girl, I'd better not go any farther," he said when we were at the bottom of Mt. Vernon Street. "Sure wouldn't want to run into Libby right now. Reckon she'd shred me with her teeth if she saw me with you." He made a biting gesture and grinned.

I laughed. "I doubt that," I said. "Well, she would be surprised," I couldn't help saying.

"What about you? What do you say about me?"

"I always thought that you were the best kind of uncle a girl could have. You swung me about the backyard by my ankle and wrist and you called it flying—"

"*You* called it flying," he corrected. "I called it exhausting."

"And you sent me a perfect silver armadillo necklace for my eighth birthday." I lifted my chin and touched the armadillo. "See, I still wear it."

He held the armadillo. I could feel the back of his warm fingers on my throat. It made me swallow.

"Girl, it's been years since I sent you this. How long has it been?"

"Ten years."

"You've kept it ten years?" He seemed incredulous.

"I've *worn* it ten years," I corrected him, holding his eyes.

He looked away first. "Seems like a thousand years ago," he said, almost under his breath. He was looking at his shoes. "Well," he said, straightening himself up, "gotta go."

"There's a new movie next week, with Steve Martin in it."

"I'll try and catch it. Thanks a lot for the pass. G'night, girl." He turned and was almost running down the street. His white summer clothes shimmered in the half light.

Up in the apartment I looked in the bathroom mirror in the dark to see if it were true—if my hair did glow in the dark. And you know what? Not only did my hair glow but my whole face glowed. It was Willy's doing. I believed it with all my heart.

After that I saw Willy regularly. The Bijou ran movies that had had their first runs elsewhere and kept them only a few days. Willy always appeared at the second movie so that I could finish the show with him. He brought the pass in a plastic see-through case and showed it to Sweeney or Salvatore, and they let him in. And once he was safely in the theater, I would pay for his ticket.

I could hardly bear the intrigue of seeing him and wanted desperately to talk about him with someone. Libby was impossible. She represented the family position: Willy was sociopathic if not downright sinful. I couldn't talk to Salvatore, who didn't know anything about Willy, but still insisted, with the kind of arrogance that only the pigheaded possess, that Willy was slime. I had already told Thomas more about Willy than I had intended to—it seemed inappropriate somehow to discuss him further. That left Fiona, who, I now decided, had only been mildly revulsed by the idea of my attraction to "Uncle Willy." So when I couldn't stand it anymore, I called her, even though it was during the day and the telephone rates were at their highest.

"I found Willy," I told her excitedly after we had gone over the trivial stuff. "You know, Marianne's ex-husband."

"Your uncle? The one in your painting?"

"Yes, and he looks fabulous. He's been coming regularly to the movie house where I work, and then we go for walks. He's so nice —really!"

"You're dating him?"

I liked the sound of that. "Well, sort of," I said.

"We're talking about your *uncle* here, right?" She made him sound like head lice. "Isn't he old enough to be your dad? I mean, how old is he?"

Her interrogation irritated me. I wanted her to be happy for me and stop asking stupid questions. "No," I said. "He's only thirty-two or so." I didn't really know how old Willy was. "I've never seen a more perfect face."

"Artistically speaking, you mean."

"Artistically, romantically, philosophically—he's just handsome. Fiona, aren't you happy for me?" It was Fiona who usually encouraged me in romance, and here she was acting so uptight about it all.

"What does Libby think about your seeing him?" Six weeks out of high school and Fiona was sounding like my mother.

"She doesn't know anything about it. My whole family hates him." How could she be so dense?

"Well, maybe they have a good reason for hating him."

"He left Marianne—that's why they hate him." What could I say to convince her that Willy was okay? "They were fighting anyway," I blurted. It was true, I realized, thinking back to that scene in the backyard over ten years before. They *were* fighting. Marianne hardly spoke or looked at Willy. She was mad at him before he left. "They were fighting," I repeated.

Fiona sighed at the other end of the line. "My parents fight all the time, but my dad doesn't leave," she said. "Fighting isn't any excuse to *abandon* somebody."

She sounded so self-righteous. I couldn't believe it. "He's very nice to me," I said, but my voice sounded defensive and dead.

"Then there's probably nothing to worry about," Fiona said. I was sorry I'd called her. It was plain that there was no one I could talk to about Willy and me. Except Willy himself. When I really thought about it, that was the way I preferred it.

∽ *10* ∽

The biggest way to celebrate the Fourth of July in Boston is to go to the Esplanade Concert on the Charles River. That was what Willy told me. He said the Boston Pops played all this lighthearted music while people sat on their blankets on the grass and listened. And after the concert there were fireworks above the river. He said a girl like me should definitely go because I'd get such a kick out of it, and that I should go with him. He said he would bring a blanket and the food.

I was ecstatic.

Libby and Dan had invited me to go to Crane's Beach with them during the day, and I had told them I absolutely had to be back, because I was meeting some kids from work at the Esplanade and I didn't want to miss it. I didn't feel too great telling them this, because it was such an out-and-out lie. Up to now I had only made lies of omission—a premeditated silence. Now I was making up stories. It made me feel crummy, but not so crummy that I would miss going out with Willy.

We met in front of the Charles Street station. Willy carried a blanket and a full grocery bag. His face was almost as sunburned as mine. "Did you go to the beach too?" I asked him, taking the blanket to carry.

"Well, sort of," he said. We walked along the Charles River. There were lots of other people walking in the same direction. "I was in New Jersey for a few days. Atlantic City, New Jersey," he said.

"For a vacation?" I asked.

"Business mostly, but I did spend a couple of hours in the sun." He smiled. "I hope my nose isn't peeling like yours. You look a sight."

I immediately covered my nose with my hands.

He laughed and said, "Just kidding, girl, just kidding," and put his arm around my shoulder and left it there for a while as we walked along the river. I liked his arm around my shoulder. We fit nicely, walking side by side. His arm was still around my shoulder when he stopped and pointed to MIT across the river. He bent his head slightly to say something to me, and his cheek touched my hair, and I turned my face toward him instinctively, and we looked at each other, a little embarrassed, and I thought of the old dream: shortly after Willy left and after Derriere was born, I began to have these dreams about this ideal family.

There was a mother named Sally, a father named Jim, and a beautiful eight-year-old little girl with blond, naturally curly hair named Betsy. All of them dressed in white and never got dirty. Their world was the perfectly sunny world of the Impressionists. Betsy wore a taffeta ribbon in her hair and walked between her parents, holding their hands when they weren't all three riding in their white convertible with the shiny chrome bumpers. They always smiled at each other and hugged a lot. Perfect love and all.

I was Betsy in the dream. Except occasionally I was Sally, when I felt like being grown-up and having breasts and kissing Jim in a different way than a daughter could do.

It's not a dream I care to analyze, but somehow it explains the confusion I felt with Willy's arm around my shoulders. Was I Betsy or was I Sally?

Even though we were early, the Esplanade was already filling up with people. Willy insisted we sit near the front, close to the open bowl where the orchestra would sit. I followed him like a duckling following a parent between the clusters of people grouped on the lawn, trying with difficulty to avoid stepping on someone's blanket. At last Willy spotted a piece of green and dropped our blanket on it. We overlapped slightly with the people surrounding us. He didn't seem to notice the hostile glances—we had invaded their space evidently. I know I blushed uncontrollably, but Willy already sat on the blanket, pulling wrapped sandwiches out of the paper sack. "Sit down, girl," he said, handing me a sandwich.

I sat down, unwrapped the sandwich, and bit into the warm, spicy meat. "Pastrami's my favorite," I said. "We never have it at home. It's too expensive."

Willy smiled and opened up cartons of potato salad and some Italian macaroni salad with red and green things in it. He pulled out plastic forks and spoons and two giant dill pickles. Then he handed me a can of Coke, and I did this incredibly Freudian thing. I mean, I wasn't thinking or anything, and I have no idea why I did it; perhaps it was the way his hand, with the long tanned fingers, was curved around the can. I can't explain it. It was just there.

I kissed the back of his hand. I did. It was like I was unconscious. I don't know what prompted me to do it, but I wanted to be swallowed up in the earth, turned to dust and ashes when I realized what I'd done.

Willy was as surprised as I was. "Girl, I didn't know you cared," he teased.

And right then a voice overhead said, "Sue!" And when I looked up, there stood Dan with two huge carton cups of Coke from the concession stand. He had that typical grin from the side of his mouth that now seemed obnoxious, almost sinister. Had he seen me kiss Willy's hand?

"Dan!" I could hardly breathe. "What are you doing here? Where's Libby?" I was talking much too fast, like someone guilty of unspeakable crimes.

Willy bowed his head low when he heard Libby's name.

"We're here for the concert of course. We're way in the back about a hundred miles from here." He looked at Willy and then back to me. He smiled impishly, I thought. He saw me kiss Willy's hand. He did. I was positive.

"Oh," I said. "I'd like you to meet my friend from work, Salvatore Zaccardi. Salvatore, this is Dan Lavenstein, Libby's friend."

They nodded at each other.

"I've heard a lot about you," Dan said.

"Same here," Willy said. "I feel like I know you and Libby already." Willy, reluctant to raise his head for close scrutiny, seemed to be talking to the blanket.

"Well," Dan said to the back of Willy's head, "I'd better go before the ice melts." He jiggled the Cokes briefly. "Enjoy the concert," he said.

"You too," I said. "Say hello to Libby."

He nodded back to me as he stepped carefully around the people seated directly behind us.

As soon as he was gone, I covered my face with my hands and let out a muffled screech. "Can you believe it?" I whispered to Willy. I was the one feeling completely paranoid now. "Can you believe the awful coincidence of running into him with thousands of people around?"

"You thought fast, girl. That was good, introducing me as Salvatore what's-his-name. That was real smart," he said.

"I can't believe it. Do you think he believed me? I mean, that you're Salvatore?"

"He sure did."

"What if he comes back with Libby?" The thought made me physically ill.

"I don't think he will. The concert's going to begin soon." He nodded toward the stage, which was now filling up with members of the orchestra.

I craned my neck nervously to see if I could see Libby off in the distance somewhere.

"Besides, they'll lose their place if they both come trudging over here."

"I guess."

"Finish your supper, girl." He smiled. "I've been slaving away all afternoon to fix you this meal. Made this cake from scratch." He was opening a box with half a chocolate cake in it. The frosting was an inch thick.

"You and what delicatessen?" I felt more relaxed because Willy was calm.

He cut a piece of cake and placed it on a paper plate. "Now I'm going to hand this to you, and if you're going to kiss my hand again, I want you to warn me so that I don't drop this into your lap or, worse, my lap." He smirked openly.

"Willy!" Five quarts of blood rushed to my head as he set the plate down on the blanket.

"Just kidding, girl. Just kidding." He handed me a plastic fork.

"I—I—I—"

"I—I—I—" he imitated, raising his dark eyebrows playfully.

"I can't explain it," I said.

"Obviously," he laughed.

The orchestra, dressed in white dinner jackets, was now gathered on the pavilion, noisily tuning. And then they stopped quite suddenly, and the concertmaster appeared. I put down my sandwich and clapped along with everyone else. Willy continued eating his sandwich, a bemused look on his face.

I stuck my tongue out at him and continued clapping. The orchestra briefly tuned up again with the concertmaster and then grew silent. The bearded conductor appeared and the audience clapped more vigorously. Willy clapped by hitting his free hand against his thigh.

They played a series of Viennese waltzes first. It took all the restraint I could muster to keep from swaying back and forth to the three-quarter time, to keep from humming, to keep from throwing my arms about Willy's neck.

I was Sally of the dream, not Betsy. I would never be Betsy again. I was the grown-up Sally. But what did Willy see? Sally or Betsy? I wasn't sure.

I wasn't sure through the whole *1812 Overture,* through the show tunes. Sometimes I would catch him looking at me, peculiarly, as if he himself was ambivalent about my stage of maturation. I seemed to be somewhere between tadpole and full-grown frog. In any case he persisted in calling me "girl."

"Here, wear my jacket, girl," he whispered, draping his jacket around my shoulders when the fireworks started. They spread across the sky—glittering, exploding willows. Willy oohed and aahed in exaggeration with the crowd. They sounded like the *Wheel of Fortune* audience. It made me laugh. As beautiful as it all was, as relaxed as Willy seemed to be, I could not forget that Dan and Libby were somewhere in that giant, vibrating crowd of people.

"I think we should go before it's over," I said. "We don't want to run into Dan and Libby."

"No, we don't." He began stuffing things into the grocery sack, mixing perfectly good leftover food with trash. Mother would have died. "You want to walk along the river?" he asked.

"Too risky," I said. I thought for a minute. "Let's ride an electric bus. I haven't done that yet. Could we?"

"Sure." Willy pulled me to my feet. "Those electric buses really get my heart going," he said, folding the blanket. It looked like a military blanket. "Those buses are more exciting than any roller coaster I've ever been on." He smirked. "I especially like the way they have those electric antennae like giant bugs. I like that feeling of sitting inside of a giant praying mantis. Those electric buses—"

"Willy!" I slugged him in the arm.

"They won't let old people on those buses, because it's too exciting for their feeble hearts." I followed him through the crowd of squatters. "And they certainly don't allow babies on those buses, because it takes their breath away and they die. As a matter of fact at the entrance to the electric bus there's this yardstick, and if you're shorter than the yardstick, you're not allowed on the bus, because it's just too dangerous. Midgets can't ride the electric bus, because their little feet dangle on the bench, and they get thrown around the bus because of the motion." He turned suddenly, and I bumped into him. "Let's see if you're even tall enough to ride an electric bus." He laid his flat palm on top of my head. "Don't know if we should take the chance," he said. "You're barely three feet tall."

"Willy!" I said, removing his arm from my head. "We don't have to ride the electric bus—"

Then he laughed and pulled me to him and hugged me hard and said, "Girl, you're so much fun to tease."

No, I would never be the little girl, Betsy, again. I was glad to be grown up and hugging Willy. I liked hugging him more than anything I could think of. I liked the feel of his body.

We rode the electric bus up Commonwealth Avenue, past Boston University, past Boston College even, all the way to Newton. It took a couple of hours to get up and back. Willy told me about playing jump rope with his sister, Ella, in Dallas, "a hundred years ago" and recited rope-skipping songs to me. He even got up and demonstrated jumping red-hot pepper in the aisle of the bus, until the bus driver yelled at him to sit down or he'd kick him off. I laughed so hard that he yelled at us again.

The only verse I could remember had to do with kissing:

> Cinderella
> Dressed in yella
> Went upstairs to kiss her fella
> How many kisses did she get?
> One, two, three, four, five . . .

Willy walked me all the way up Mt. Vernon Street. We stood away from the streetlight. "I had so much fun," I said. "Thanks."

"Me too," he said. "I'm just crazy about those electric buses."

I laughed. "I'd like to invite you over for lunch sometime when Libby is at work, okay?"

"That'd be nice," he said. "It'll have to be in a couple of weeks, because I'm going out of town on business again."

I wanted to ask him about his "business" but felt intuitively that he would not want me asking, so I didn't. "You're coming back again, aren't you?"

"Well, sure, girl. I said in a couple of weeks."

"How will I know when you're back?"

"I'll come by the Bijou and see you." A glint came into his eye. "I'll let you kiss my hand all you want," he said.

"Are you going to kid me about that forever? I—I—I—"

"I know, girl. You didn't know what you were doing." He reached for my hand and kissed it twice. "You owe me one." He smiled. "G'night." He strolled off down the street, the blanket folded under his arm, his hands in his pockets.

I doubted that I would ever have another Fourth of July as wonderful as the one I spent with Willy. I wondered if Marianne remembered holidays with him. Or had Heber filled the empty space Willy left? Is that possible?

11

One day when I returned home from work around dinnertime, I could hear Grace bawling upstairs—even from the lobby. I skipped the mailroom and ran all the way up the stairs. "Grace?" I said.

She sat hunched at the top of the stairs, crying, her hands and hanky covering her face, her gray hair wet and matted against her forehead.

"What is it?" I sat down next to her and felt immediately helpless. "What's happened?"

"Priceless is dead," she wailed, dropping her hands. Her face was wet and so distraught, it shocked me. "My Priceless is dead."

"But this morning he was fine," I said.

She nodded. "He ate raisins from a spoon and jumped through the quilting hoop this morning. He was as good as he ever was. Then we took a little nap. I lay on my bed, and he lay at the foot of the bed like he always does, and when I awoke, he was dead. Oh, Priceless!" She began crying noisily all over again.

"Come inside with me," I said, pulling on her arm. "We can talk." She leaned heavily on me as we walked down the hall. I unlocked the door and led her into the living room, where we both sat on the sofa.

"What am I going to do without my little Priceless? I have nothing. Nothing." She weaved back and forth on the sofa and wiped the tears from her face.

"You're *sure* he's dead? I mean, did you call a vet or anything?"

"I know a dead dog when I see one." She moved away from me. "He hasn't moved for four and a half hours now. Even Priceless can't play dead that long."

"Maybe he's comatose."

She looked at me as if I were a complete idiot. "He's dead," she said. "Believe me."

"I'm sorry," I said. I realized I should have said that some time ago. "I really am sorry. I'll help you bury him if you like."

"I'm not sure I can bury Priceless," she said.

"Cremate him?" I asked.

"I could never do that," she said.

I couldn't think of any alternative, so I said nothing.

"I'm thinking of having him stuffed by a taxidermist," she said quietly.

"You're kidding," I breathed. I had never heard of anyone stuffing a dog before.

"It might be too expensive, but I'm going to think about it a couple of days and then decide."

"I don't think you should leave the dog lying around for a couple of days." I wanted to say that he would "spoil," but I didn't want to offend her again. "If he's dead, then . . ." I hesitated, "then he needs to be *disposed* of in some way—soon." There weren't enough good euphemisms to cover this subject.

"He'll be all right in the freezer," she said briskly. She wiped her face with the hanky again. "At least until I've made up my mind."

"The freezer?" I'm sure my mouth hung open.

"I can't just leave him lying on my bed. He'd gather flies. And I can't decide about having him stuffed just yet. My brain is addled, having him gone. I can't think clearly."

"It sounds like you've thought of just about everything," I said.

She stayed a few minutes longer and then left in a flurry, saying she had to make some phone calls and do some comparison-shopping for taxidermists.

WHAT LIBBY SAID WHEN I TOLD HER THAT GRACE WAS THINKING OF HAVING THE DEAD PRICELESS STUFFED: "I think a chestnut dressing would be nice."

WHAT DAN SAID: "Stuffed into what? Will he have wheels attached so we can pull him around the hardwood floors? Will he squeak when you push on his tummy?"

WHAT LIBBY SAID WHEN I TOLD HER GRACE HAD PRICELESS STORED IN HER FREEZER: "You mean like prom flowers or the top of the wedding cake?"

WHAT DAN SAID: "I think we ought to cover him with meringue. Instead of baked Alaska, we'll have baked bow-wow."

WHAT THEY BOTH SAID WHEN THEY FINALLY GOT SERIOUS: "Poor Grace."

A few days later Grace came pounding down the door. "Sue, are you there?" she yelled, her fists thumping. "Sue!"

"What, what, what?" I opened the door.

She stood, hands clasped under her drooping bosoms. "The *David Letterman* show called me," she said, grinning coyly. "They want me and Priceless on their show. They really liked that video film you made."

"You're kidding."

"Priceless would be so proud," she said, rocking on her toes.

"You told them, didn't you? I mean, you told them that Priceless was—"

"Dead as a stone," she finished.

"Oh, what rotten timing. It would have been so much fun for you—"

"They don't care if he's dead. They said they wanted me anyway, and they'd just run the video, and then Dave and I could talk about it."

"*Dave* and you?" I laughed.

"They'll pay for me to stay in a hotel and everything. It's going to be a real vacation." She crossed the threshold and squeezed me. "Thank you," she said. "You are my best friend."

I wanted to object: "You're an old lady. I can't be your best friend," but she was hugging me.

"The painting of Sean will be ready for you when you get back," I said. "It will be a kind of celebration present."

"Next week is going to be a good week, then," she said. "I'm going to go back and tell Priceless all about it." She started for her apartment.

"I'll be glad to take care of your place while you're gone," I said. "You could leave me a key and—"

"No thanks," she called back. "I'll just be gone a couple of days."

She wasn't ever going to let me see her apartment. I wanted to see the mounds of stuff: the saved letters wrapped in yellowing ribbon, the grape-jelly glasses, the rows of Coca-Cola bottles. I wanted to see all of it.

I wanted to see my future: an aged eccentricity that reached way beyond what was chic.

～ *12* ～

Dad always used to say that he might never have gotten married if it hadn't been for Mom's High Lemon Pie. That snagged him, he said. I didn't really believe him. I mean, that old myth about the way to a man's heart being through his stomach is just so stupid. Who would bother?

I would. I invited Willy over for lunch when he returned from wherever he'd been. We met in the Isabella Stewart Gardner Museum on the Fenway. I didn't know what the museum was all about. I mean, Libby had mentioned to me a couple of times that I ought to go there, but it hadn't registered in any serious way. So when Willy and I met in "Mrs. Jack's" house—that's what they called old Isabella—I was stunned. The whole house was built around this magnificent formal garden about three times the size of our house in Springville. The sunlight poured through the gigantic windowed ceilings three stories above onto the Venetian walls and balconies, onto the marble statuary, onto the summer flowers blooming profusely below, onto Willy in white, hands in his pockets, leaning against the side of an archway, waiting. Waiting for me.

First I saw the painting of the two Spanish dancers by John Singer Sargent that was displayed prominently just inside the front door. The flaming red of the woman's dress attracted me, but as I moved in closer, an archway to my right opened into the garden court, and I turned my head and saw it all, the garden, the light, the marble, and Willy leaning and waiting. And it was in that perfect visual moment that I knew I wanted to marry him.

I knew his faults. I knew that he probably didn't hold jobs for long. I knew he would disappear for weeks without notice. Maybe he even gambled. I didn't care. *I* would work. *I* would pay our way. There would be no demands, only that he would always come back to me.

Willy kissed my cheek when I greeted him. "Hello, girl," he said.

"Hi," I said, not able to meet his eyes. Just knowing that I wanted to marry him made me shy. "This is like being in Europe," I whispered. "At least what I imagine Europe to be like."

"It is very European," he said.

"I like the feel. I like the feel of Europe."

"You should go there. I'll be your guide."

"Would you?"

"Sure." He led me across the tiled court toward the stairs.

"I'd like that," I said. The thought of being in Europe with Willy made me dizzy. It could be a honeymoon, I thought.

We walked the stairs, both of us in white, like two ghosts in a dark hallway—we floated up—up the stairs of Isabella's house and drifted through the Dutch room, and though I nodded at the paintings, and though we spoke of them and chatted with a guard briefly, I remember none of them. I only remember Willy in white, the smell of musk, and the way he leaned toward me when we talked. I knew a Rembrandt was in the room, but I wasn't looking.

On the third floor we stood in front of Titian's *Europa and the Bull.* It covered one whole wall. The bull had lifted Europa into the air with its head. Her limbs were flung out, her head turned to us with a look of—not fear really, not even real anguish—with a look of surprise, as if she hadn't realized there was even a bull close by, until it caught her up with its horns. Even though it was only a painting, I wanted to save her.

"She looks so forlorn," I said to Willy.

"The bull doesn't look none too happy either," Willy said. "I'll bet you paint as good as that," he said.

"Not as good as Titian," I said.

"I'd like to see your work."

I wondered why he hadn't gone to Swinton's Frame Shop to see my paintings when they were there. "Why don't you come to lunch on the fifteenth. Libby has to be at a shoot for a commercial on that day, so she won't be home." I didn't tell him it was my eighteenth birthday too. "I have all the paintings there now."

"You sure?"

"Positive. She's been complaining about it for days. I'll tell her I'm having Salvatore over."

He smiled.

"I'll make High Lemon Pie," I said.

"That sounds mighty fine," he said in that soothing voice.

We turned back toward the stairs, but I couldn't help turning to catch a last glimpse of Europa, *surprised* by the bull.

Dan came to eat late supper and watch Grace's television debut on the *David Letterman* show. He mixed salad at the kitchen counter while Libby poured tomato sauce over a tray of spaghetti and began arranging meatballs on top. "Would it be okay to have Salvatore over for lunch before I go? He's been so nice to me. I thought I'd invite him on my birthday when you have the shoot."

"Isn't this guy a little old for you?" Libby wiped up some splatters of spaghetti sauce from the table with the edge of her apron.

My face got all hot. "Well, it's no big deal, because we're only friends. I mean, I'm not planning to marry him or anything."

"I wasn't worried about that," Libby said.

Dan grinned out of the side of his mouth and took his glasses off and wiped them with a paper towel. "I agree, it shouldn't matter.

After all," he said to Libby, "you're much older than I am, and it doesn't bother us a bit, does it?"

Libby looked up from her spaghetti platter briefly. "Sure, hold that three and a half months against me. Anyway, you're not seventeen going on eighteen."

"I'm really not interested in Salvatore except as a friend," I said. "There's nothing to worry about."

"Friends?" Dan mouthed the words at me in silence and raised his eyebrows incredulously. He began kissing his own hand passionately, though silently.

I glanced at Libby to see if she was catching this pantomime, but she was carefully placing parsley on each side of the spaghetti platter.

"That was nothing," I said to Dan. My face was burning up.

"What was nothing?" Libby asked.

"Nothing," I said.

"Nothing was nothing," Dan said. He was grinning into the salad he was now tossing.

"Let's eat, then," Libby said.

"Please," I said.

"Saved by food." Dan grinned at me as he set the salad bowl down on the table.

After dinner and cleanup Libby rolled the TV and VCR out of her bedroom and into the living room. We had promised Grace we would copy the show. The three of us sat on the sofa watching a late-night *Magnum, P.I.* rerun, our shoeless feet spread across the coffee table. The story line had to do with some teenage girl who has a wild crush on Magnum and is always calculating ways to be with him; she finally kisses him. Dan tapped my foot with his and, looking over the top of his glasses at me, said, "There's something familiar about this plot."

I ignored him.

"You've probably seen it before," Libby said.

"I believe I have," he said. He had this idiotic smirk on his face.

Finally David Letterman came on. He announced the "Stupid Pet Tricks" and even said Grace's name, but then we had to wait through a commercial and through Dave yukking it up with the band leader, Paul Schaffer, and then through Dave walking backstage to see what Hal, the director, was wearing and then through another commercial. Finally he announced Grace McGregor from Beacon Hill in Boston, and out she came wearing this navy-blue print dress with the pockets for raisins and the white collar. Instead of walking directly to Dave, who stood behind his desk, she looked straight into the camera and waved and then waved at the audience, grinning like a beauty queen.

"She's been waiting all her life to do something like this," Libby said. "This was a great idea, Sue."

I nodded nervously. "You don't think she'll say anything about having that dog in the freezer, do you? She's not that out of touch, is she?"

"Yes, she is," they both said.

"I understand your dog isn't with you today; is that right?" David Letterman asked Grace.

"He's dead," Grace said. "He died in his sleep."

"That does present a bit of a problem, all right," Dave said. "What was his name?"

"Priceless—his name was Priceless."

"I hope you won't be offended at my asking this, but what do you do with a dead dog on Beacon Hill in Boston? I mean, you probably don't have a backyard to bury him in. Do they have pet cemeteries, or what?"

"Here it comes," Dan whispered under his breath.

"Right now he's in my freezer," Grace said quite matter-of-factly.

David Letterman hardly flinched. "Uh-huh," he said. "The freezer."

Grace turned in her chair slightly. "I'm thinking of having him stuffed, but I needed time to think about it, so I put him in the freezer," Grace said. "I didn't want him to gather flies," she said.

"Makes perfect sense to me," Dave said. The audience was going crazy. "Is there anything else or *anybody* else in your freezer, or is Priceless in there by himself?"

Grace thought for a moment. "I've got some Weight Watchers fudge bars in there and a boneless ham."

Dave just smiled his gap-toothed smile while the audience retched around with this information. "Is there any chance that you would confuse the ham with the dog?" he asked.

"The dog has fur," Grace said.

Dave leaned forward and patted Grace's knee. "Of course, I should have thought of that," Dave said. "Well, are we ready to see the video?"

Libby, Dan, and I were rolling over each other with laughter.

"Can I just say who made the video film?" Grace asked.

"Sure," Dave said.

"My best friend, Sue Smith, made the video. She lives down the hall from me."

I almost wanted to cry when she said that, because really I had given Grace so little of myself and she was calling me her best friend. It seemed so sad. I was glad I had done the portrait of her son.

"Good, let's have a look, then," Dave said. Priceless appeared like a dog raised from the dead to jump through Grace's arms and through the hoop and to eat raisins from a spoon. He really was a pretty cute dog, I decided.

When Grace began reciting Gray's "Elegy," they broke to a commercial. When they came back, Dave Letterman thanked Grace for coming on the show. "Good luck with finding a taxidermist," he said. "And I hope they don't have any power outages in Boston this summer." They shook hands. Grace blew kisses to the audience and waved at them, the loose skin of her upper arms flapping wildly. The audience clapped as if she were a rock star. Finally it was over.

Dan turned down the sound. "That was too much," he said, wiping his eyes with a handkerchief.

"Incredible," Libby sighed.

"She was a star," I said. "A shining star."

I could tell that Dan and Libby wanted to be alone for a while, so I rolled the TV and VCR onto my porch and watched the tape about a hundred times from my bed. The painting of Sean was drying under my bed, and I reached down and pulled it out. I had made him look like a god. Grace would love it. I shoved it back under the bed and pulled the finished full-length portrait of Willy out a little ways. "Good night, my love," I said softly and pushed it gently back under the bed. I turned off the light and went to sleep.

∽ *13* ∽

Libby got up earlier than usual on my birthday so that she could fix me Belgian waffles on her "machine," as she called the waffle iron. I didn't have the heart to tell her that I wasn't hungry. I was nervous/excited/anxious/ecstatic that Willy was coming. All of the above. I wanted to get up and dance on my toes, whirl about the room like a top, sing an ethereal song. I wanted to beat my breasts and howl like Tarzan. Still, I waited patiently in bed as Libby had ordered and waited for my birthday breakfast, humming not the birthday song but "The Wedding March."

"Happy birthday, dear Susan, happy birthday to you," Libby sang in her off-key voice and carried a mountain of waffles cluttered with eighteen flaming candles.

"Make a wish before you blow them out," she ordered. "Make it a good one."

I closed my eyes and wished for a life with Willy. No one in my family would have approved. I blew out all the candles with one breath.

"Did you wish to stay in Boston?" Libby asked, helping me pluck out the candles.

"Sort of," I said, spooning raspberry syrup on the waffles.

"Sort of?"

"In order to get what I wished for, I'd have to stay in Boston," I said.

"I see," Libby said. "I think." She left the room briefly and returned with a large gift-wrapped box, which she set on the bed. "This is from Dan and me," she said. "I'm really sorry we can't do more on your birthday, but next weekend we'll go to the beach."

"I'm having a great birthday already," I said. She held my plate while I unwrapped the present. It was very heavy. "Must be gold bricks," I said, removing the tissue from the top of the box. "Oh, Libby, it's wonderful. It's so perfect." I lifted out a terra-cotta statue of an armadillo set on a wooden block.

"You seem to have this thing for armadillos," she said. "Dan bought it in South America."

"I love it. I love it so much," I said. It reminded me of Willy, and I loved anything that did that. "It's beautiful," I said. And it was. I got out of bed and placed it on my desk, moving it around to see which view I wanted to have of it. I ran my hand across the ridges of its back. "It's so lovely," I couldn't help saying again.

"I'm glad you like it. I've got to go now. I won't be back until late. Will you be all right?"

"Perfectly," I said. "Thanks for the breakfast."

"You're welcome. Enjoy yourself with Salvatore," she said.

"I will," I said. I felt like a sleaze for lying to her.

"Happy birthday again." She rummaged through her briefcase, blew kisses at me, and said, "I'd give anything to be eighteen again" as she left the room.

"Life begins at forty," I called to her.

"Tell me about it," she yelled back. The front door to the apartment opened and slammed shut.

I spent the morning picking up Libby's clothes, which were strewn around the apartment, vacuuming, scouring the bathroom, setting my paintings, which now included the *Family Portrait* and *The Woman in the Straw Hat* and others I had shown at Swinton's, against the cupboards in Libby's kitchen. Periodically I checked the refrigerator to see if the Herbed Spinach Bake and High Lemon Pie, which I had prepared the night before, were still intact. The inside of the refrigerator looked strangely like Mother's. I set the table using the terra-cotta armadillo as the centerpiece, then sat down and pretended to talk with an invisible Willy. "Yes, I'd love to marry you," I said out loud. "Darling."

Darling is an embarrassing word to say aloud. I don't know anyone personally who uses it except when referring to kittens or talk show hosts. I decided never to say it again, although I did spend most of the morning talking aloud to Willy-the-fantasy, saying the most clever things, until Willy-the-real-person arrived at noon on the dot. When he rang up, I raced downstairs to the lobby to open the door for him.

"Hi," I said breathlessly. "You're right on time."

"You said noon, didn't you?"

"Yes, but I—I—I—you know!"

Willy looked dazzling in white. He imitated my speech. "I—I—I. Something happen to your tongue, girl?"

"I—I—I. No!" I laughed. "At least I don't think so. Come on up." I took his hand and led him through the lobby.

Willy blew a low whistle through his lips. "This is some place. Libby must be making big bucks."

"She does all right, I guess," I said.

He followed me into the mailroom. There were a few bills for Libby, but there were three boxes for me wrapped in brown paper and a letter from Thomas. Derriere had printed "Happy Birthday" with different colored magic markers all over the packages.

"Let me carry those," Willy said, taking the boxes from me. He inspected them carefully. "When's your birthday?" he asked me.

"Today, actually." I led the way to the stairs.

"Girl, you never told me it was your birthday," Willy said. We climbed the stairs together.

"I didn't want you to feel like you had to bring me anything."

"What would have been the matter with my bringing something?"

"Nothing. It's just that I—I—I—"

"There's that I—I—I again." He grinned.

I unlocked the apartment door and let him in. "Whooey, this is quite a place," Willy said. He set the packages down on the grand piano. He looked all over, ran his hand along the porcelain bowl with the figures dancing in bas-relief around it, and ran the toe of his shoe back and forth across the Persian carpet. "Mighty pretty," he said.

"You like pretty things, don't you?" I said. "It's one of the things I remember about you when I was little. You had a good eye."

He took my hand and kissed it lightly. "That's why I like you," he said. "You're by far the prettiest thing in this room."

"Stop teasing," I said.

"Girl, is someone teasing?"

"I think the casserole is ready," I said, and walked into the kitchen.

I was doing exactly what you're not supposed to do, and what you never do when you're having a fantasy. You never cut the beloved short when he's telling you you're gorgeous while kissing your hand. Never. But I couldn't stand it for too long in reality, because I'm really not that pretty. I mean, I'm symmetrical and all, but I'm not exactly beautiful and far from gorgeous. Just symmetrical, and my hair's thick. It helps to have thick hair. I don't want anyone lying to me. That's a funny thing for me to say, when I've been lying my face off all summer, but it's the truth.

Willy was the really gorgeous one in the apartment. "Your paintings!" he exclaimed as he walked into the kitchen. He lifted some of the smaller ones up and then stood in front of the *Family Portrait*. "I'm in it," he said, a little astonished, I think.

"Yes, I still consider you part of the family."

"This Heber?" He pointed to Marianne's smiling partner.

"Yes."

"He's a good man, you say?"

"Yes."

Willy nodded. "They're all really fine paintings," he said. "I'm so proud of you."

I thought of the dream where I kept switching from being the child-daughter, Betsy, to being the mother-wife, Sally. When Willy said he was proud of me, I suddenly switched to being the niece-girl, Susan. I didn't want to be her at all. Not now. Not on my eighteenth birthday, when I was finally of age—of marriageable age without having to ask anyone's permission.

"Thank you," I said.

The spinach casserole with the cheese and bacon was ready, and I brought out the fruit salad and the poppy seed dressing, which I had made from scratch, and we ate it all and didn't die.

Willy pushed his chair away from the table and leaned back, sighing, "Girl, you cook as well as you paint. That was real tasty, but I still don't think it's fair that you're cooking for me on your birthday. You should have let me know. I would have taken you *out* for lunch. I feel bad that I didn't know it was your birthday."

I gathered up the plates and set them in the sink. "This is what I wanted for my birthday—to have you over for lunch." I rinsed off the plates and opened the dishwasher. "I wish I didn't have to go to work this afternoon."

"Don't go!" Willy said. He slapped his hand down onto the table. "You don't have to go. It's your birthday, for heaven's sake." He slapped the table again. "Come away with me this afternoon."

I turned around. Willy's face gleamed. Everything about him was so perfect. I had thought so all my life.

"Where would we go?" I asked. I was terrified and hopeful at the same time that he would reply, "Let's go get married. You're eighteen now. You don't need anyone's permission."

Instead he said, "We could go to the beach. Not Crane's Beach, with all those deer flies. We'll go up the coast to Maine—Ogunquit. Ogunquit will be perfect in August."

I was both relieved and disappointed. "I haven't been to Maine yet. I have a friend who comes from Maine—Thomas. Libby was going to take me one weekend, but then I had to work and—"

"See how work is always keeping you from having fun," he said. "Put those dishes away, and let's go to Maine." He stood up and danced around the table in a kind of jig. "Let's go to Maine. Let's go to Maine. Let's go to Maine on Susan's birthday!" He sang it like a child's rhyme. He grasped my hands and swung me around in circles about the kitchen in a kind of dance, all the time singing the chant, "Let's go to Maine on Susan's birthday." The way he held on to my hands, the way we circled, the way we sang—for I was singing it too—reminded me of long ago when Willy—Uncle Willy then—swung me around the backyard grasping hands and feet and allowing me to fly. I felt so light then, so full of possibility. And I felt that way again, dancing in Libby's kitchen: like I was light as the particles of silver dust that float through the window at twilight.

And then we hurled into the refrigerator. And I was reminded that I was made of flesh and blood and bones. We laughed too loudly. "I don't think anybody was leading," Willy said.

I rubbed my arm above the elbow.

"Are you hurt?" Willy asked. He rubbed my arm, and our fingertips met briefly.

"It's only a bruise," I said, looking into his face. And then I did something I felt old enough to do now. I put my arms around Willy's neck and kissed him on the lips. It surprised him momentarily, so that he stood there like a mannequin, stationary, but then he grasped me around the shoulders and pulled me in close to him and kissed me back. It was my first true kiss. Those kisses with Brian Chamberlain in the school gymnasium while *The Electric Horseman* flickered on the screen in front of us were cardboard kisses. They were nothing.

"Girl," Willy murmured, pulling away slightly.

"Willy, I'm not a girl." I leaned into him. "I'm not a girl, Willy."

We kissed again. I loved kissing Willy.

The phone rang, a jarring, obtrusive, unwanted ring. I broke away reluctantly. "It might be Libby," I said. "She knows I'm here." I picked up the phone. It was Salvatore.

"I got real trouble," he said. "That slime, Zella, hasn't shown up. And I can't get ahold of Sweeney or Jill. I've been running the concession myself. You've got to get down here."

"It's my birthday," I said lamely.

"Sue, give me a break. I'll make it up to you. I'll buy you a Gucci watch for your birthday. I'll bake a cake with a naked man in it. Anything, but please get your bod down here. It's Saturday afternoon and the place is filled with teenyboppers. I can't handle it alone."

"I'll be right there," I said.

"Tanks," he said, and hung up.

I held the phone in my hand and looked at Willy.

"No beach?" he asked.

I shook my head. "Salvatore's alone, and the place is a zoo. I have to go early."

Willy shrugged and smiled. "What time do you get off?"

"I could leave at ten." I hung the phone receiver in its cradle.

"How about if I pick you up, and we go have one of those Steve's Ice Cream sundaes you're so crazy about? It'll be a birthday sundae."

"That would be terrific—something for me to look forward to." We stood looking awkwardly across the room at one another. "I love you, Willy." It felt brave and grown up to say it aloud like that directly to his face.

"Girl—Sue, don't—" The slightest flinching of a muscle altered his face.

"I know you're a lot older than me, but it doesn't make a stick of difference to me," I said. He looked so pained. "Does it bother you that I'm so young?"

He seemed to be thinking about his answer. "No," he said finally. "It doesn't bother me in the least." The splendid mouth grinned suddenly. "I think you're something else." His eyes wavered to his shoes. At that moment I felt older than he. "Let's go," he said. "I'll walk you to work."

"I've got to get my man-made fibers first," I said, dashing into the closet on the porch and returning with my uniform over my arm. "Let's go," I said.

He followed me to the front door of the apartment, and when I put my hand on the doorknob, he covered it with his and kissed the back of my neck. I turned the knob, and we were out in the hall. I locked the door with my key while Willy kissed my neck again.

Despite the hot August heat we walked clutching each other down Charles Street, and when we got in the Common, Willy made up a game. He would say, "See that tree down there, just beyond where the woman is standing with the stroller? When we get there, I'm going to kiss you." As the game progressed, the tree stops became more frequent. I was having a superior birthday.

On Washington Street Willy pulled me close to a building, out of the way of the pedestrians.

"Let me take the armadillo necklace," he said. He was smiling in a secretive kind of way.

"Willy—why? I've never taken it off in ten years. Never!" I emphasized.

"I'm not going to keep it." He crossed his heart. "Promise."

"But why?"

"It's a surprise," he said. "A birthday surprise." He reached for the latch at the back of my neck, but I twisted away from him. "Okay," he said. "Listen."

I stopped writhing.

"I want to take the necklace into Shreve Crump and Low's and have them make a bracelet that matches the necklace exactly: same chain, same armadillo—for you. Let me do it." He smiled. "For your birthday."

"That's a lovely idea," I said. "It's too expensive, though."

"You're worth it," he said, releasing the clasp. He placed the necklace in his shirt pocket.

In front of the Bijou Willy stopped short. "Dammit," he said. "I left my jacket at Libby's."

"It's hanging on a chair in her kitchen," I said.

"I've got to get it. It's got my wallet in it. We don't need Libby finding that in her kitchen."

"I'll go back with you," I said, turning.

Willy surveyed the line of kids forming down the block. "You can't," he said. "Salvatore will have a fit if you don't show up soon."

I reached down into my handbag for the key to Libby's apartment. "You go get it," I said, handing the key to Willy.

He turned it over in his hand. "I don't know . . ." He faltered. "I feel funny about being in Libby's apartment without you there."

"You're only getting your jacket, for pity's sake, and you can give it back to me tonight."

He smiled sheepishly. "Okay," he said. He closed his fist tightly around the key. "I'll meet you here, in the lobby, at ten o'clock on the nose." We kissed one last time. "Happy birthday, sweetie," he whispered.

I watched him as he dodged pedestrians down the sidewalk, hoping he would turn and wave at me, but he never did.

⤞ 14 ⤝

Salvatore greeted me when I walked in the door. "Boy, am I glad to see you," he said. A swarm of kids lusting for junk food hovered noisily about the concession stand. I had to shove some of them aside to get in. "I owe you one," he said, handing popcorn and a Coke to a girl.

"I'd like to get off at ten instead of ten-thirty tonight," I said, slipping into my jacket. "Willy's going to take me for a sundae."

Salvatore nodded as he counted out change to the girl. "Okay by me," he said.

For twenty minutes we hustled Dots, Pom Poms, Nibs, and candied almonds to the hungry hordes. Finally the movie began, and the traffic in the lobby slowed down to a trickle. Salvatore stopped helping customers and began straightening the stock. I fixed myself a Coke and sipped it between customers.

"So, Sue," Salvatore began. He was scooping popcorn carelessly into the medium-sized sacks. "You still seeing that funny uncle of yours? What's his name—Whoopy?"

"Cute," I said. "Real cute."

He grinned broadly, still scooping the popcorn. "You know, if you go for that kind of guy—I have this uncle myself, who, by the way, is *younger* than your uncle and who plays the horses—he could show you a real good time."

"Shut up, Salvatore." It came out nastier than I intended.

Salvatore flinched and blew air between his full lips. "Whew, you really like this guy, don't you? I mean, this is getting serious."

"Yes," I said softly. "I'm going to marry him."

He dropped the sack half-filled with popcorn into the bin and came and stood by me. In a lowered voice he asked, "You're going to marry him? I mean, has he asked you?"

"Not yet, but he will."

"How do you know?"

I looked into my Coke. "I just know."

"Has he done anything to you? I mean—"

"No! He's just been very nice to me. He's always been wonderful to me. Why does everyone always want to bad-mouth him?"

Salvatore shrugged. "I don't really know the guy. I'm sure he's a very nice guy." He smiled at me. "I apologize," he said.

"Okay," I said.

He walked back to the popcorn machine. "I just don't like his face. He has a slimy face," he muttered.

"Salvatore!"

He lifted both his hands up. "Truce. I call truce."

"If you don't have anything nice to say, then don't—"

"Please, keep those Utah platitudes to yourself. I'll keep my mouth shut, and you keep yours shut." He grinned at me. "If I'd known you were a Sunday-school freak, I wouldn't have hired you."

"Promises, promises."

We had a full house all afternoon and evening. The movie was one of those hysterical teenage horror films: blood and guts and more blood and guts. Salvatore and I would burst out laughing when the sound of the chain saws started up. Mostly girls, but some boys too, would come streaming out of the double doors gasping for a few minutes of reality. When the noise of the chain saws ended, they'd peek through the little windows set in the doors to see if it was safe to go back to their seats.

Around dinnertime Zella finally called in to say that she had the flu and had slept right through her scheduled time to work. "That's fine, Zel," I heard Salvatore say. "Get well. And next time call me."

The memory of Willy's kisses wafted in and out of my head a thousand times during the evening, lifting my otherwise routine chores to a sublime level. The memory was textured with feelings I hadn't felt before that afternoon—a kind of bubbling joy—a kind of excitement. I thought it was love.

At nine forty-five, when the last show had begun, Sweeney, his jacket slung over his arm, stood solemnly in front of the concession stand and started singing "Happy Birthday" with his hand over his heart as if he were singing "The Star Spangled Banner" or "God Save the Queen." Salvatore marched in with the saddest-looking little cake I'd ever seen with a single, oversized candle pressed through its center like a stake. "Happy birthday, dear Susan," the two of them crooned. "Happy birthday to you."

"Oh, an Italian cake!" I said. "How sweet."

"With an Irish candle," Sweeney said.

"Cut the crap and cut the cake," Salvatore said, handing me a plastic knife. I cut it into four pieces, placing each piece carefully on a napkin. Sweeney took a huge bite out of his immediately. "Tastes better than it looks," he said with his mouth stuffed full.

"It's chocolate," I said. "So it can't be all bad."

"Go right ahead and insult this cake. Be ungrateful. See if I care," Salvatore said.

"I love the cake," I said. "Don't get all Italian on me."

"What are you gonna do now that you're legal?" Sweeney asked. Crumbs were stuck all over his mouth and chin. He ate like a slob. "Want any suggestions?"

"She's going to become a famous artist and get married this

year," Salvatore said. He raised his piece of cake. "Cheers," he said.

"Sounds like a contradiction to me," Sweeney said. He shoved the remaining piece of cake into his mouth—he ate the whole piece in three gulps—and wiped his face with his jacket.

"I plan to be perfectly happy," I said. I wrapped the remaining piece of cake tenderly in a napkin for Willy.

"Go for it," Sweeney said. "There's my brother. G'night you guys. Happy birthday, Sue." He opened the front doors and disappeared into a blue van.

While Salvatore stood by eating his cake, I began straightening the booth.

"You don't have to do that. You can go now," Salvatore said.

"It's all right," I said. "Willy's meeting me here. I'll just putz around until he gets here."

He shrugged. "I'll be in my office. I need some coffee to help wash this block of brown down."

"You said it, not me," I said.

He smirked and walked across the lobby.

I had so much energy, I felt I could spit-shine the entire theater in five minutes. I hustled about the booth cleaning spills and replenishing candy where needed in the display. Inside my head this ridiculous childhood chant kept repeating itself: *Susan and Willy, up in a tree, K-I-S-S-I-N-G.* It was another rope-jumping rhyme. *How many kisses did she get: one, two, three . . .* She got as many kisses as she could jump "red-hot pepper." My face grew hot when I realized that the rhyme was playing itself over and over again in my head like a stuck record on an old phonograph. *Susan and Willy up in a tree . . .* I had kissing on the brain. Delicious kissing. Kissing Willy again and again.

When I looked up, it was ten fifteen, and Willy had not yet arrived. By ten thirty there was nothing left to clean, so I sat on one of the benches lining the lobby and twitched my foot back and forth to the music in my head: *Susan and Willy . . .* Willy's wrapped cake nested in my lap. *Up in a tree . . .* Sometimes I got up to see if a lingering figure in front of the theater was Willy, but it never was. *K-I-S-S-I-N-G.* At ten minutes after eleven the last movie ended, and a couple of hundred people streamed through the lobby and out onto the street. I looked for Willy among them. Maybe he had come in when we were busy and watched the movie. Willy liked movies, and he was so forgetful about time—as free spirits often are. There were a couple of Willy look-alikes that made my heart jump, but no Willy.

Salvatore had come out of his office to see the people out of the building and to check the theater and rest rooms for any strays. "There's always some bum trying to spend the night in the the-ater," he had told me when I first began working there.

"So, Sue, are you still here?" he asked me, coming out of the theater. He had turned off the lights, and it now looked like a black cave.

"Yeah. I must have heard wrong," I said. "I was probably sup-posed to meet him at Steve's Ice Cream, and he's probably sitting there right now, all finished with his hot fudge sundae mad as . . ." I waited while he checked the men's john.

"Mad as hell," Salvatore yelled from inside the john. He turned off the lights and came out. "You can swear now. You're eighteen."

"Yes, that mad." I swallowed. "He'll come around tomorrow and want to know where I was and why I didn't meet him. He'll say something like—"

" 'Where the hell were you anyway?' Something like that?" Sal-vatore checked the cash registers one more time to make sure there was no money in either of them.

"Yeah, and I'll feel so foolish having waited for him here . . ."

"For an hour and forty-five minutes," Salvatore said. He practi-cally spit the words.

"Has it been that long?" I asked feebly.

"He's not coming, Sue. My bet is he won't be here tomorrow

either, or the day after that, or the day after that. The guy is a genuine slime."

"That's not true." I thought about the perfect afternoon with Willy. "It can't be true." I stood by the front doors while Salvatore set the burglar alarm. The lights in the lobby were off now, and only the streetlight lit the front of the theater. We stepped into the warm August night. "I'll drive you home. It's too late for you to be walking home by yourself." He checked the doors after he locked them. I followed him down the street to the parking lot. In the car I stuck the wrapped cake I was still clutching into my bag.

"You want me to drive past Steve's Ice Cream?" Salvatore asked, putting the key into the ignition.

I could have kissed him. "Oh, would you mind? I'd be so grateful."

He breathed a deep sigh, as if to say it was all hopeless. I reached for the silver armadillo at my neck, like I always did for luck, but of course it was gone. Willy had it—to make a matching bracelet for my eighteenth birthday. The Boston Steve's was closing as we drove up. There was one table of people finishing their ice cream, and that was all. Willy was not among them.

"Maybe he meant the Steve's in Cambridge," I said softly.

Salvatore pulled away from the curb. "Hey," he began. "I once had this Irish setter named Dutch. That is, I had him for a while. He didn't really belong to anyone but himself. Anyway he showed up on our porch out in Dorcester, his tail wagging like he'd loved me all his life, and my mom said I could keep him. I was so excited. I bought him a special bowl for his food with his name in green letters on the side, and a water dish. He'd run alongside my bike when I did my paper route. He had this deep red coat. He was a cool dog." He turned the car onto Storrow Drive toward Cambridge. "When he'd been with me for three months, he—"

"Is this a metaphorical story?" I interrupted. "I mean, this lovable dog of yours disappears, right?"

"Well, yeah, but—"

"Did he come back?"

"But that's not the point of the story, see."

"Did he come back?"

"No, he never did, but something real interesting happened to *me* because—"

"I don't want to hear about it," I said.

"Sure, at first I was disappointed, but then—"

"It's not the same, and I don't want to hear about it," I said. "It's not at all the same. Not a bit."

We drove in silence. The arc lights along Storrow and Memorial drives were reflected in the Charles River, distorted, as if you were seeing them through tears.

Salvatore took the Boylston exit and crossed the bridge. The gold dome of Harvard's Eliot House glittered darkly in the moonlight. "I have to let you off here; no cars allowed in Harvard Square," he said. He had pulled up to the curb. "I'll wait here until you get back." He slumped down into his seat as if it was going to be a long wait.

I ran through the block to Massachusetts Avenue. The lights still blazed in Steve's, and I could see that people were seated inside. Couples lingered in the plaza where I had first met Willy. I ran across the street and grasped the door handle. It was locked. I knocked on the door and pressed my face to the glass.

"We're closed, lady," one of the guys shouted from behind the bar.

I knocked again and gestured for him to come to the door.

"We're closed," he shouted again, but seeing my gesture, he walked reluctantly around the bar and opened the door. "Read my lips," he said. *"We are closed!"*

"I know," I said, gasping. "I just need to know if there was a man here tonight around ten o'clock."

"Lots of 'em."

"No, a tall man, in his thirties, with dark, wavy, almost curly hair, wearing white slacks and a white shirt and a taupe linen jacket and leather sandals."

He shook his head.

"He would have been sitting alone, like he was waiting for someone."

"I don't remember. Really, I don't." He had dropped the sarcasm. "Look, it's a hot Saturday night in August. Everybody and his dog has been in here tonight for ice cream. Unless he was wearing a chicken suit or a beanie with propellers, we just didn't notice who came by. Sorry." He smiled.

"Thanks for your time," I said.

I walked back to the car. Willy could have been detained at his work, I thought to myself. If he worked. I had no idea what Willy did with his time, or where he lived, even. It wasn't that I hadn't wanted to know, but I'd always felt instinctively that those were questions that Willy would not want me asking, so I hadn't.

Salvatore dropped me off in front of Libby's.

"Thanks a lot," I said through the open car window. "You're a real friend."

"Yeah, I'm a regular sweetheart," he said. He pulled away from the curb and disappeared up the street.

I had given my key to Willy, so I had to ring up to the apartment so that Libby could let me in. "I forgot my key," I said through the intercom. She buzzed me into the lobby. When I reached the fourth floor, the apartment door was open for me, but the apartment was completely dark.

"Libby?" I called, standing on the threshold.

"I'm in here," she said from the living room.

I closed the door and felt my way down the hall. Something was wrong. The air smelled of tobacco for one thing. But something else was wrong too.

I could see Libby's dark form lying on the sofa. The air was thick with tobacco.

"You can turn on a light," she said. "I've just been lying here smoking."

I clicked on a lamp next to the sofa. Libby blew smoke into the already tobacco-hazed room. I was astonished. "You don't smoke!" I said.

"I never have up to now, but one of the detectives left a pack on the coffee table, and I thought this was a good time to try it." She sat up slowly and tapped the ashes of her cigarette into a lotus bowl.

"Detective?"

"I was robbed today."

I surveyed the room for the first time. All the oriental rugs were gone. The etchings, the porcelain bowl with the figures.

"Your paintings are gone too," Libby said. She snuffed out the cigarette and waved her arms to clear the air.

I ran into the hall, turned on the overhead light. The floors and walls were entirely bare. Not one of my paintings rested against the kitchen cupboards as they had earlier that afternoon, when I showed them to Willy. I leaned against the refrigerator. Afternoon had been so long ago.

On the table lay a single key. My key. I held in my stomach, which felt sick, with one fist and grasped for the necklace that I knew wasn't at my throat and never would be again. "He stole the armadillo too." I whispered. Tears burned behind my eyes.

"Yes, I feel so bad about it." Libby stood in the doorway and, seeing me clutch my throat, realized that I meant Willy's necklace and not the terra-cotta sculpture.

"Sue," she said, gripping both of my shoulders. "Where was your necklace? I thought you always wore it."

"I *was* wearing it, and I gave it to him." I felt like I was strangling. I looked straight into Libby's eyes. "I gave him the key too," I said.

"Who, Sue? Susan? Who?"

"Willy," I said. "Uncle Willy."

15

Libby tried to listen about my meetings with Willy all summer, but she kept interrupting: "Are we talking of Willy Gerard here—that Willy?"

"Yes, Uncle Willy."

"But he's forty!"

Now I was in shock. "He is? I thought he was thirty-two."

Her eyes narrowed. "Did he tell you that?"

"No, but—"

"Sue, he was thirty when he left. He'd been a pilot for years before that."

So Fiona had been right when she said Willy was old enough to be my father. She had called me perverse. Now I felt perverse. I continued spilling my guts out.

"You paid for all his movies? Why? They're only a dollar. Couldn't he afford his own dollar?"

It did seem chintzy now that I thought about it.

I told her about the events of the afternoon and really stunned her: "You were actually thinking of *marrying* Willy?" Her shocked expression—the wide eyes, the dropped mouth—caught me off guard.

"He—he was so nice," I stammered.

"Nice? *Nice?* Where have you been all your life? He stripped down our whole family. He abandoned Marianne. He discarded her and took everything they owned with him. He's not *nice,* Sue. He's a smiling barracuda. He's human slime." She squeezed my arm for emphasis.

"That's what Salvatore said," I told her, dropping my head down. It was hard to look her in the face.

"Well, Salvatore was right." She let go of my arm and turned slightly, her fingers rubbing her forehead as if searching for answers. "I don't get it," she murmured. "How could this have happened? You knew about him. You were there . . ."

"I was only seven—"

"But you saw what he did to Marianne. She lived in your basement all those years."

"Yes, but . . ." I was still backed up against the refrigerator.

"You saw how she hurt. You couldn't have missed that, even at seven. We all talked about him. You couldn't have missed the talk. Surely it was clear—"

I wanted her to stop pressing me that way, as if she blamed me. Louder than I meant to, I said, "She was mad at him when he left. Marianne was mad at him." I met her eyes.

"What?"

"She was mad; I can remember that. She was hardly speaking. She was tired of going all those places: Kuala Lumpur and Sydney, Australia. He touched her hair. He didn't want her to be mad at him, but she wouldn't look up or talk—"

"What are you saying?" Libby's voice was low, but intense.

"I don't know. Everyone always blamed Willy, but Marianne didn't seem to want him that day. She didn't want to go with him, I don't think."

"Are you saying she deserved to be abandoned?"

I had to stop and think. "She didn't want him and he left," I said. I had believed this all my life, I realized. The refrigerator motor started up a loud humming. The vibrations warmed my back. Libby and I stared at each other for what seemed like hours.

"So why did he leave you?" she asked.

I didn't know.

"Why did he steal everything in sight, including all your work from the last two years?"

I clenched my jaw to keep from crying.

Seeing I had no answers, Libby turned away and surveyed the stripped hallway. "All my stuff—all my adult life's possessions— taken by that sneaky bastard." Her shoulders stooped in a way that made her look her age, made her vulnerable in a way I didn't really want to see.

"I have to see Dan." Her voice grew decisive. "I've got to talk to an *adult*."

That stung.

She grabbed her handbag off the table. "He's working late at his office," she said without looking at me. Her heels clicked along the wooden floor. "Don't wait up for me."

With my fingers I tried to rub out the incredible headache raging behind my temples. I would have given Willy any paintings he wanted. He didn't have to steal them. I would have given him a lifetime of paintings. Why did he go?

On the porch I wandered in circles, feeling ashamed. I didn't cry. It was walled up somewhere behind my eyeballs. I didn't cry. All my life my family had told me that Willy couldn't be trusted, and I had trusted him instead of them. I had told him I loved him. Once the phone rang, and I hoped it was Willy: "I've done the most foolish thing, girl—" And that made me feel even more ashamed, to think that I still hoped to prove all the familial voices wrong. Willy wasn't going to call now or ever.

A stray birthday candle from that morning's waffle cake lay on the bed, reminding me that it was still my eighteenth birthday. It made me more determined than ever not to cry.

I slept a thick, heavy, deathlike sleep and didn't wake up until I heard Libby's and Dan's voices in the kitchen. By then it was noon. They had sent out for Chinese food for lunch, and Dan insisted that I join them in the kitchen. He stood in the doorway. "Get up now and eat something," he said.

I sat down, still dressed in a nightgown, my hair uncombed, opposite Libby. She shoved a white carton of egg rolls across the table. Dan placed one on my plate. "At least eat an eggroll," he said. Normally I loved egg rolls, but today they smelled disgusting.

Libby and Dan heaped all kinds of stuff onto their plates from various white paper cartons. Libby ate silently, sighing occasionally as if she was exhausted. Our eyes never met. Dan made several suggestions for how they could spend their afternoon. Libby, her voice tired, said, "That'd be okay," to every single suggestion. She looked about as depressed as I felt.

"I'll pay you back," I finally said. "If it takes my whole life, I'll pay you back."

Libby looked up briefly and then took a bite out of her eggroll. "On your salary," she began with her mouth full, "it would take a lifetime." It sounded pretty icy and made me feel worse. She sensed this and waved me off with her hand impatiently. "Never mind about it—I'm insured—you don't owe me any money. Just forget it now."

"It was my fault. I gave him the key so that he could come back for his jacket."

"You didn't know he was going to steal everything in sight," Dan said.

"She should have," Libby muttered under her breath, but I heard it quite plainly.

"I didn't know," I insisted. "Maybe he'll bring it back. I mean, maybe he'll think about it and change his mind and bring it all back. He'll apologize and—"

Libby and Dan exchanged a look.

"I guess not," I said. The shame of what I had done washed

over me in a new wave. "I feel so terrible about everything," I said.
"I feel so ashamed." It helped to say it aloud.

"Look, let's not talk it to death," Libby said. "It's done, and
blaming yourself won't get you anywhere, and besides, it's boring."
She looked at her plate when she said this.

Dan cleared his throat. "Now *that* is a sin," he said. "Boring
Libby is a sin."

"Well, I apologize for that too," I said.

Dan smiled, but Libby rolled her eyes up in her head, not bothering to hide her disgust: "Please stop apologizing all over the
place. It's nauseating."

"I'm going to get dressed," I said, pushing my chair back.

From the porch I heard Dan say to Libby, "Lighten up a little,
why don't you?"

And I heard her say to him, "Bite yourself, why don't you?"

I stayed on the porch alone for the rest of the afternoon. It was
obvious that my presence irritated Libby. For the first time that
summer I felt unwelcome in her apartment. It was depressing. I
opened the birthday presents my family had sent me, hoping for a
little relief, leaving the letter from Thomas unopened on my desk.
I would save it for later. Derriere had bought me another one of
those glass-ball paperweights with the snow in it. He had already
bought me three of them. This one came from Disneyland with
Mickey Mouse standing inside dressed in winter clothing and
holding a snowball. Derriere had scrawled in crayon, "I know you
like these—Love, Derek." *He* was the one who liked them. Mother
and Dad sent me a wool cardigan cable-knit sweater they had paid
too much for. Mother had written a note saying I could use it for
school in the fall. They were expecting me to come home. I wasn't
sure what I should do anymore or where I belonged.

The last present was a two-pound box of Cummings chocolates,
all of them dark, because they were my favorite. Maybe they
would help appease Libby a little. I carried the box into the living
room, where she and Dan were playing backgammon. "Let's eat

the whole box this evening," I said, shoving the open box in front of them.

"Ah, I see signs of recovery," Dan said. "Thank you, I think I will." He plucked a dark chocolate mound from its paper cup.

Libby took two. "One for each side of my mouth," she said. She smiled at me without malice. "Thanks, Sue," she said.

I felt a whole lot better.

Grace was due back from New York on Monday morning, and I fully expected to meet her in the hall on the way to work, but she wasn't there.

Salvatore didn't ask me about Willy, and I didn't tell him about the robbery. He spent the afternoon entertaining me with Steve Martin imitations, and I dutifully laughed at all of them. It was exhausting, having to pretend to be happy. Exhausting for both of us.

On the walk home I looked for Willy on Washington Street, on the Common, on Charles Street, on Mt. Vernon Street. I hoped he would pop out from behind a tree or a building and say, "Surprise! That was some trick I played on you, wasn't it? I'll bet old Libby's ready to quarter my parts."

When I was almost home, I turned around and walked all the way to Boylston Street to Shreve Crump and Low's, the jewelry store, and asked the man in the dark suit behind the counter if they had a silver armadillo necklace they were holding for a Mr. Willy Gerard. "He was going to have a bracelet made to match it," I said.

The man disappeared into a doorway and returned shortly. "I don't see it," he said. "When would he have brought it in?"

"Saturday afternoon or this morning," I said.

"I don't have any record of it at all," he said.

"Thank you."

*　　*　　*

Willy, how you burn behind my eyes. How you smart. Your kisses have turned to cold sores and boils. Your smile scrapes my insides. I am only eighteen. You should have known better. I am only eighteen. I am a humiliated eighteen. I was no match for you. I am so young. Only eighteen.

When I got home Libby was already there, opening her mail at the kitchen table.

"You're home early," I said.

"Dan and I are driving out to the Wayside Inn for dinner in a few minutes. I need to get away from this place for a while."

I wondered if she meant she had to get away from me.

"A Detective Crawley from the Boston Police Department was here just a few minutes ago to see you. He said he'd drop by this evening again. I think he wants an up-to-the-minute description of Willy the Creep."

"Okay." I headed toward the porch to change my clothes.

"What the hell is this?" Libby's voice exploded.

I turned. "What?" I asked.

"This phone bill!" She thrust it at me. "Almost three hundred dollars' worth of calls to Springville, Utah. Did you also let Willy use my telephone?"

That ticked me off. "No, I didn't, and you don't need to be so sarcastic."

"I'll be as sarcastic as I damn well please. Were you planning to pay this or just sneak off"—she hissed it—"to college and hope I didn't notice?"

"Of course I was planning to pay it." Actually I had no idea that I had called Fiona that often and for that long a time. It was her phone number listed on the long-distance bill. "I am not a sneak," I insisted.

"You haven't proven it by me," she said. "I want the three hundred dollars right now." She extended her palm as if I had three hundred dollars in the pocket of my uniform.

"I'll get it tomorrow morning out of my savings account."

"I'd rather have a check right this minute," she said, her stupid palm still extended.

"I don't have a checking account; I only have a savings account."

She withdrew her palm. "Tomorrow morning—first thing."

"Yes, ma'am." I was pleased to see her flinch slightly at the *ma'am.* "May I be excused now?"

"Gladly."

I walked onto the porch and sat down on my bed. Libby said the S-word out in the kitchen and then left the apartment, slamming the door shut much louder than usual.

"Same to you," I said aloud. Did I even have three hundred dollars in the bank? I couldn't remember. I felt like a mess. I decided to open Thomas's letter now. He always made me feel better. I moved to the wicker chair and pulled three thin pieces of airmail paper out of the envelope with Thomas's beautiful writing on them. The margins were filled with wildflowers, painstakingly watercolored, unspeakably lovely. "Your pressed forget-me-nots inspired the motif for the margins," he wrote. "Am very glad that my margins with fish didn't inspire you to send me a pressed cod," he continued cheerfully. My whole tense body began to relax. He was loving Italy, the painting was going well, and someone wanted him to illustrate a book on fish, which he thought he would do, because "As you know, I am very much into fish." He said my sketches of Grace and Priceless were sensational, and he thought a fine painting would come of all of it.

"But," he wrote, "I feel less sure of your sketches of your Uncle Willy. Does he really look like that? Is he that square-jawed, and do his eyes gleam in quite the way your highlights suggest? Is his hair that thick, that curly? Do his muscles shine like the photographs in those muscle-mania magazines? I feel reluctant to ask these questions, because I saw your portraits, Susan, saw your clear vision of other people, and have faith in that vision, but I have to say, quite honestly, that the sketches of your Uncle Willy seem distorted to me and therefore false. You make him look like He-Man."

I gasped and laid the letter in my lap. His observations seared. I felt dismayed and hurt. I stood up and walked around the room, but there was no real escape. Thoughts raced in my head: *You make him look like He-Man. You make him look like He-Man. He-Man. He-Man. He he he he hee hee hee.*

It was a relief to hear the intercom buzzer, to answer it. Detective Crawley was waiting down in the vestibule. I pressed the button to let him in. I still carried Thomas's letter in my hand and returned to the porch and laid it on my bed. I would finish it later, when I had more strength.

Detective Crawley had a flat-top haircut and looked like an ex-marine. I let him into the living room. "I talked to your aunt, but she suggested that you might have more information about"—he looked down at his notebook—"Willy Gerard."

"I was the last one to see Willy," I said, "and can give you the most current description, but I don't really know much. He never told me where he lived or what he did for a living. I know that once this summer he went to Atlantic City. He said it was on business."

Detective Crawley scribbled as I talked.

"Did you find his fingerprints on the key?" I asked.

"Yeah, we found his prints. We just can't find him. Where did you meet this guy?"

I told him about meeting Willy by accident in Harvard Square and then told him about all the other meetings. "It's not much help, is it?" I said.

"You have a picture?" he asked. "We've got a fifteen-year-old air force snapshot to work from, but that's it."

I shook my head. "Wait," I said. "I have a painting of him. It's big, though. It's under my bed."

He wanted to see it, so I walked down to my porch and pulled it out from under the bed. The painting I had done of Sean Mc-

Gregor slid out with Willy's painting. I had painted Sean's cheeks pinker than they ever could have been in real life, had reddened his lips and whitened his teeth, had made him handsome as a god, the way I knew Grace wanted to remember him. I had distorted the portrait for Grace because I cared about her.

I stared at Willy's portrait. He was in white, standing with his hands in his pockets. He was tanned and muscular. Too muscular. He looked as if he had baby oil rubbed all over his arms. His cheeks were too pink, his teeth too white. He was as handsome as Sean McGregor and a god. Who was I distorting him for?

I knew the answer. I said the S-word. *The Incredible Hulk,* I thought. *Superman,* I thought. *He-Man!*

I picked it up and turned to carry it out of the room, when I noticed for the first time that Thomas's watercolor, the one that said "See you in September," was no longer hanging above my desk. And I knew that Willy had taken that too. It was too much. "No!" I shouted. "No, no, no!"

"Miss, are you all right?" Detective Crawley called to me. He was standing halfway into the hallway.

"No, I'm not all right," I yelled. "He took a watercolor of mine. It was a present from a friend. I just now saw it was missing." I walked down the hallway dragging Willy's portrait, which thumped rhythmically with my footsteps along the wooden floor. "Why would he take that? He's not going to get any money for it. It has more sentimental value than artistic value. Why would he take it?"

I was barking out the questions so loudly that Detective Crawley took a step back to give me room for venting. "He's just a thief, miss; he's not an artist," he said. Truth spoken by a detective.

I set Willy's portrait against the grand piano and sagged into a nearby chair. "People have been trying to tell me that all of my life," I said. I smiled feebly at him.

"That's him?" Detective Crawley stared in disbelief.

"It's a little idealized," I said. "Actually it's a whole lot idealized, but take away the makeup and that's him—sort of. He did wear those clothes all the time. He always wore white."

Detective Crawley nodded and then took several snapshots of the painting with a small camera he had with him. "If these don't work, I may have to come back. Thanks for your help. And you may find other things missing—people usually do. Just let us know."

I showed him out the front door, then returned and stood in front of Willy's portrait. I felt like throwing up. I thought of all the time I had spent working on this excruciatingly embarrassing work of nonart. Thomas had seen right through it.

"Schmuck!" It was directed at the portrait. I yelled other words incorporating several very fine alphabet words creatively linked together. And when words failed, I kicked my foot right through the canvas until my leg hurt and I had to sit down.

He's just a thief, miss; he's not an artist. It smarted to think how I had thought Willy was an artist, because he listened to me once when I was seven years old—listened to me explain about a painting of him without asking me any questions about my arithmetic. I was the one who had turned him into an artist, because *I* wanted him to be one. *I* wanted it. Mother had called him a jerk, a parasite, a sociopath. She had called him irresponsible, untrustworthy, and shiftless.

And now, sitting in Libby's bare living room, looking at the brutalized canvas, I realized for the first time that Mother had been right all along. MOTHER WAS RIGHT. GRANDMA WAS RIGHT. All the grown-ups had been right on this one. They were right; I was wrong. Pigheaded and wrong.

Was I wrong about becoming an artist too? About living in Boston? I argued with the adult voices in my head:

—*Teaching art is one thing, but living an artist's life is not possible.*

—*But that's the only life I want.*

—*No one can live on art alone.*

—But there are people who do.
—No one we know does.
—Thomas's family lives by their art.
—How long have you known this family? What do you really know about them? You need to be more realistic about your life. Be realistic, like we are. You haven't sold one painting this summer. Not one.
—I don't want to live like you.
—Come home now.
—I want to live here. This is my home.
—You can't be trusted to do the right thing. You don't even know what the right thing is.
—Maybe I'm deceiving myself again.
—For sure.

Waves of anxiety knocked the breath right out of me and made my arms tingle and feel weak. My ears buzzed. Maybe the adult voices really did know all. Maybe I didn't—couldn't—know what was best for me. I rocked back and forth, holding in my middle, trying to make the anxiety go away. *What if the adults knew more about me than I did?*

I threw up in the bathroom. In bed I lay with my knees pulled up to my chin, the covers over my head. Adult ghosts plagued me with their whispered advice: *Come home. Go to school. Get married. Raise a family. Die. Just like everybody else.*

Libby's muffled voice, rising into laughter from the kitchen, woke me. At first I thought she was talking to Dan but, not hearing a second voice, realized she must be on the phone. I concentrated on pushing down the anxiety rising in my throat.

"Sue, are you awake?" Libby stood over my bed.

"Yes," I said.

"It's your mom on the phone. She wants to talk to you."

The digital clock on the table next to my bed read 1:10 A.M. "Now?" My voice was husky.

Libby turned on a lamp. She was still in her street clothes. "I suspect she waited until after eleven to save money," she said. "She says we're never home in the morning when she calls."

"I am," I said. I felt heavy and dull getting out of bed. I wondered if Libby had told Mother about Willy and me, about the robbery. I could hardly breathe.

Libby followed me into the kitchen, where she sat down to read the *Boston Globe,* which was spread out all over the table.

"Honey, did I wake you?" Mother's voice was cheerful. She didn't know! "I know Lib stays up all hours of the night, so I thought I'd chance it."

"No, I was awake." I could breathe now.

"You haven't written anything about your plane reservations, and your dad wants us all to go camping for a few days before you go to school—just down to Bryce and Zion's—but we need to know when you're coming, so we can plan around you."

"Oh, yeah, well, I—I—" *I could tell her now. I could just say it: I could say that I'm not coming home.* "I haven't made the reservations yet," I said. "I've been sort of busy." *Busy chasing Willy around Boston.* Libby must have been thinking about the same thing, because she looked up briefly and shook her head.

"Sue, school starts in just a little over two weeks . . ."

"I know—I know it does. I'll call the airlines first thing in the morning. Really."

"I hope it's not too late . . ."

"It'll be fine. I'll call you tomorrow night and tell you when I'm coming." I let out this huge sigh that surprised even me. "Okay?"

"Call after eleven; it's cheaper."

"Yeah, I'll call after eleven."

The beginning of a smirk edged Libby's lips.

"You okay? You sound kind of tired."

"Mom, it's past one o'clock in the morning here."

"Oh, yeah, forgot about that." She snickered. "Take care, then. I love you. And I'll hear from you tomorrow night."

"Yeah. Love you too. 'Bye." I returned the phone to its cradle.

Libby's head remained bent over the newspaper.

"Thanks," I said, "for not telling her about Willy and me and everything."

She looked up. "You're welcome, but I did it partly to protect myself. I was afraid she'd think I hadn't taken very good care of you this summer." Libby, I realized for the first time, felt responsible for what had happened. She felt guilty.

"You weren't supposed to take care of me, remember? We made a deal." I pulled out a chair and sat across the table from her. "I was supposed to take care of myself."

"So was my goldfish." Her face was cupped in her hands, and she smiled a little. "And it ended up in the toilet."

"I'm not a goldfish."

She sighed. "No, you're not a goldfish." She folded a section of the paper and set it aside. "I came down pretty hard on you this afternoon about the phone bill—"

"I should have kept track," I said quickly.

"I didn't have to be nasty."

"I didn't have to be irresponsible."

"Truce?"

"Truce."

In bed I lay thinking about the possibility of staying in Boston. I couldn't stay with Libby—I had shot that wad. But I was pretty sure I could stay with Zella for a few weeks, and if not, the newspaper was filled with ads for people wanting roommates. I could get a better-paying job and save money and go to art school after I had established residency. I could do that. Mother wouldn't think it was a good idea. Just like she wouldn't have thought dating Willy was a good idea, and she would have been right. The anxiety rose in my throat again. I probably shouldn't even be thinking about it. I went to sleep positive that I was insane.

❧ 16 ❧

First thing in the morning Salvatore called to ask if I would help him with some bookkeeping before the theater opened. He was in his office when he called, so I showered quickly, dressed, and met him down there. He sat at his desk with an adding machine while I read columns of figures to him. It was all supposed to add up to some predetermined figure, and when it didn't, we'd begin the process over again. During a break, while eating day-old popcorn (or month-old—it tasted kind of dusty), which Salvatore stored in his office, I said, "I'm going home soon, you know."

"What's the attraction?" Salvatore was still convinced that Utah was a planet "unto itself," as he had said many times.

"It's home, stupid."

"So is Beirut for someone. That doesn't mean you have to live there."

"Springville, Utah, is nothing like Beirut. It's much more . . ." I hesitated. "Benign," I said.

"Springville, a benign place to live. That's real catchy."

"It's very pleasant," I said.

"Springville, a far-from-unpleasant place, benign, without disease. Pack your bags, America."

I threw a handful of popcorn at him. "Shut up now. I want to tell you something."

He snorted, pleased with himself, and leaned as far back as the chair would allow. "So tell me," he said.

"Willy turned out to be a real slime." I said it slowly, thoroughly. "You were right all the time."

Sometimes Salvatore could be so classy. He didn't say one word. There were probably a million smart remarks that came into his head, but he didn't say anything.

I told him about the robbery.

"They should hang him by the—"

"They won't find him. The FBI's been looking for him for ten years for deserting the air force and who knows what else."

"You knew that?"

I nodded.

"Well, Mrs. Lincoln"—his voice turned mocking again—"except for that robbery, how did you enjoy your eighteenth birthday?" He rocked in his chair.

"He definitely was a slime."

"I'm sorry I was right about him," Salvatore said.

"Me too," I said.

Grace waited for me in the hallway when I got home. "Where have you been?" I asked her. "I thought you were coming home Sunday night." It seemed like a hundred years had passed since she was on the *David Letterman* show.

"I stayed an extra day," she said excitedly. She grabbed my arm and leaned into me as if she was about to tell me a secret. "I had lunch at the Plaza," she said in a low voice. "I hadn't eaten there in forty years. I thought, 'What the hell?'" She covered her mouth with her hand when she laughed. She wore the same crepe dress she had worn on the *David Letterman* show.

"You deserved a lunch at the Plaza," I said. "You were simply

terrific. Libby and Dan and I watched it together. You were a star."
I squeezed her arm.

She smiled and kissed me smack on the cheek. "You are like a
daughter," she said. I could tell from her face that she was serious.
"I told Dave all about you," she said. "Off the air, I mean. I told
him how it was all your idea. I told him how you were like a
daughter to me. He said to say hello to you." She patted my cheek.

"That's nice." I liked the idea of being Grace's relation. "I have a
surprise for you." I said, unlocking the apartment door.

"Is it Sean's painting? Is it finished?" she asked eagerly.

"Yes, it's finished. Sit down on the sofa, and I'll get it."

Grace looked bewildered. "Where is everything?" she asked,
looking around. "Libby isn't moving, is she?"

"Oh, no," I said. "No, there's been a robbery. It happened last
Saturday night."

"In this building?" She seemed truly alarmed. "We haven't had a
robbery in this building for years." She stood in the doorway of the
living room.

"Don't worry about it, really." I tried to soothe her. "It wasn't
done by a stranger. I mean, well, he turned out to be a stranger,
but I thought I could trust him with the key. I didn't expect that
he would, that is—"

"*You* gave him the key?"

"Yes, he used to be my uncle. The robber, I mean."

"Libby's ex-husband? I didn't think Libby had been married."

"No—no, another aunt's ex-husband. Anyway he had a key, so
it wasn't really a break-in as such."

She sat down on the sofa. "Oh," she said. Willy's portrait, with
several holes kicked into it, still lay on the floor beneath the grand
piano. "Is that Sean's portrait?" she asked, alarmed all over again.

"Oh, no, that's my uncle Willy," I said. I wished I had trashed it.
"It fell off the piano," I said. I went and got Sean's portrait from
under the bed and brought it to Grace. "I'm sorry I didn't have it
framed," I said, handing it to her.

She held it with outstretched arms, away from her body. "That's him," she breathed. "That's my Sean. That's exactly how he looked. It's beautiful." She set it down on her knees and wiped her eyes with one hand. "That's my Sean," she said again.

I was embarrassed because, like I said, no one could look the way I had painted him. He was too good-looking. No one looked like that. He was a fantasy. I should know.

"You want to watch some television with me and have some pie?"

She looked around. "Is it all right with Libby?"

"Sure. She won't be home for a little while." Actually I didn't know this, but I didn't really care either. I rolled the TV in from Libby's bedroom.

Alex Trebek was beginning the double-jeopardy portion of *Jeopardy!* "I like this program. Leave it on this channel," Grace said.

I went into the kitchen and cut some pie that I had bought on the way home from work. When I returned to the living room, Grace had fallen asleep, her head rolled slightly to one side. I set her plate of pie on the coffee table and ate my own piece and watched *Jeopardy!* This one guy was cleaning up the whole board. He already had more than ten thousand dollars.

When I finished the pie, I went and got a sketch pad and began drawing Grace lying there, a half smile on her face, clutching Sean's portrait. The final category was "Presidents." I sketched fast, afraid she might wake up and be offended at my drawing her. Her apartment keys, held together on a ring, lay in her lap. I had a momentary evil desire to snatch them quietly and go look at her apartment, but I restrained myself.

"Who was Grover Cleveland?" was the correct question, and the hotshot player won seventeen thousand dollars. I stopped to watch Alex Trebek shake the players' hands. I have noticed that he never talks to the losers, only the winners. When it was over, I turned off the TV and continued drawing Grace. In her sleep she snorted and shifted her body, the keys in her lap falling to the floor.

"Grace?" I said. "Grace? I have your pie here. It's chocolate. Grace?"

She snored gently. Carefully I picked the ring of keys up off the floor. It wasn't hard to find the one to her apartment. It was the same shape and configuration as Libby's key. I clutched it alone in my fist, letting the other keys slip down the ring. "Grace?" I called again.

She grunted and smacked her lips together and continued snoring gently. Sean's portrait now lay flat in her lap, and her hands lay limp by her side, the palms turned up.

I would let her sleep.

I tiptoed lightly into the hallway. Standing in front of Grace's apartment door with her key in the lock, I twisted, and her door snapped ajar. I took a deep breath and glanced down the hall at Libby's open door, listening for Grace. Nothing. I wondered if Willy had held his breath, or if stealing into people's homes was second nature to him.

My own heart was racing, and I felt excited, high. I pushed the door deeper into the hallway and realized almost immediately why Grace's apartment had always seemed so dark: She had a black curtain hanging from floor to ceiling across the front hall just inside the door. I pushed the curtain, which hung on a wire, to one side and turned on the light switch. My breath caught in my throat. The long, narrow hallway leading to the kitchen was a golden archive of *National Geographic* magazines. They were fastidiously stacked against the walls from floor to ceiling, their yellow backs facing the center of the hall. It was quite pretty, really—all that yellow interrupted with tiny black print announcing Zimbabwe and New Zealand. The narrow path of wooden floor was polished to an immaculate sheen. To the left I could see dimly into the living room, which was larger than Libby's and seemed to be filled with oversized furniture. The doilies, crocheted and white, neatly arranged on the arms and backs of the overstuffed chairs and sofa, were not the first thing I saw when I turned on the living room lights. It was the walls—a collage to Sean's memory—that I saw first: his army uniform, complete with medals, tacked above a side table. Between the hat and the collar of the uniform Grace had pinned an eight-by-ten glossy portrait of Sean's face, giving the effect that he had been flattened right against that living room wall in his army uniform. Other clothes, too—a pair of boy's over-alls, a winter coat with wooden buttons and a hood—covered the walls. The coffee table held different sizes of boys' shoes, from baby to high tops to a black army-issue-type boot. Did the army return his boots? A side table was filled with empty orange Nehi bottles, the caps held in a small basket next to them. Under the grand piano lay wooden sleds, one with a little seat and strap in it —the kind that might hold a toddler—and a Flexible Flyer sled with partially rusted runners. On top of the piano were boxes of games neatly stacked according to size: dominoes, Pit, Rook, checkers, Treasure Hunt, Monopoly, and, oddly, a paint-by-num-ber box. The piano bench held a suspended bridge made from an erector set.

What surprised me was the tidiness of this collection. It was clutter, yes, but it was tidy, well-dusted clutter. It was like all collages: planned clutter. When I turned to go back to the hall, Sean's report cards, framing the doorway, greeted me like old Christmas cards.

The kitchen was wallpapered with Sean's yellowed letters, his bleached handwriting barely visible. Grace, I imagined, had memo-rized them long ago. I thought of Thomas's letters pinned care-fully above my desk. The top of the refrigerator held more than half a dozen cookie jars and above the fridge on the wall hung an electric clock in the shape of a cat whose eyes moved back and forth with the passing of seconds. The kitchen table was pushed against a wall that had mismatched plates hanging above it, twelve of them, in a perfect symmetrical square. Several cups of pencils sat colorfully on the counter. Stacks of old *Saturday Evening Post* magazines lined the wall under the windowsill. I recognized the Norman Rockwell, John Clymer covers. The lampposts of Mt. Vernon Street twinkled through the window. Willy had kissed me under one of them. Was it still summer?

I sat down on one of the two chairs by the table and looked into the blank eye of Grace's old RCA console TV with the rabbit ears on top. Next to it lay Priceless's collar and his water dish and a Kerr jar half-filled with chocolate-covered raisins.

I knew I shouldn't have come.

"Robbers! There are robbers in my apartment!" Grace was yelling out in the foyer. "Help, robbers." She seemed to be yelling down the stairwell.

I stood up, mortified. I wondered, fleetingly, if I could climb out the kitchen window and jump four stories.

"Robbers!"

"What the hell—" It was Dan's voice from downstairs.

"We're coming," Libby called.

I could hear them hurrying up the stairwell. I heard doors opening and closing. I was paralyzed.

"I think there's a robber in my apartment. The door's ajar, and I never leave it unlocked. Never." Grace's voice wobbled with anxiety.

"My door's open too," Libby said, breathlessly. "You don't suppose Willy came back—"

"No." Grace interrupted her. "Susan and I were in there watching TV, and I fell asleep . . ."

"Where's Susan now?" Libby sounded truly alarmed.

"I'm here," I called, and sprinted through the golden arches of *National Geographic*s out into the hallway. "There's no robber. It's only me," I said feebly. "Here." I handed Grace's ring of keys back to her.

The three of them looked at me as if my nose had just fallen off.

"What were you doing in there?" Grace's eyes practically burned a hole in my head.

I felt completely ashamed. "I—I was curious," I stammered. "I'm really sorry. I shouldn't have—"

"Susan!" Libby's astonished mouth hung open.

"Curious about what?" Grace's voice was even. I wasn't sure how mad she was at me.

"I was curious about your place. You're always so careful not to let anyone see in. It made me want to see it even more. I'm sorry. I really am. I shouldn't have done it." I was being as honest as I knew how. There wasn't any other explanation except my idiotic curiosity to see the forbidden, but it sounded pretty cheap when I said it aloud. "And," I continued to blurt out, "I wanted to see Priceless in the freezer."

"Good grief," Dan said under his breath.

"Do you see what I've had to put up with these past few days?" Libby said to him.

I didn't say it, but I liked the juxtaposition of the dead dog next to food that humans eat. "I wanted to draw him," I said aloud. The only place I'd seen anything dead at all was on the side of the highway—usually deer or skunk. But you expected that. It was the unexpected I was after. I wondered if Eugene Stauffer had been right after all: I really was a necrophilic voyeur or at least half of that. "I think I may be crazy," I said, and believed it.

"Possibly," Libby said.

Mrs. Whitten was now standing on the stairs about halfway up from the floor below, looking through the bannister. "Was there another robbery?" she asked. Her voice had a high warble to it.

"No, it was just a misunderstanding," Dan called back to her. She looked us over with some suspicion and then crept silently back down the stairs.

"You wanted to draw Priceless?" Grace asked. She glanced down at the painting of Sean embraced to her bosom and then at the drawing notebook I was still carrying. Her voice had softened slightly.

"And you too," I said, quickly. "But I want to draw you in *your* place."

"I don't think so," Grace said.

"Why not? It's wonderful," I said. "It's a collage of your life. You've placed everything so carefully and lovingly. Why would you want to hide it behind a black drape?"

"Because"—her voice rose—"the last time I let someone into my apartment, they told everyone in the building that my place was a mess."

Libby and Dan exchanged a half-guilty look.

"But it's immaculate," I said.

"It is?" Libby couldn't help asking.

"I think you should take the drape down," I said.

"Did you see Priceless?" she asked.

"No, I wasn't in there but a few minutes."

She considered me a moment. "You still want to?"

"Yes."

"You're a strange one, you are," she said. "Come on, then." She moved into her doorway.

"I'm coming to see your dog in your freezer, and you call me strange?" I asked.

"Takes one to know one," she said, and laughed the way she used to when Priceless did a perfect doggy trick. "Do you want to come too?" she asked Libby and Dan.

"We'll pass," Libby said, pulling Dan toward her apartment. "Stay out of trouble, Sue—pleeeze." She made a warning face at me.

I followed Grace down her narrow hallway and into the kitchen, where she opened the freezer. Priceless's four feet faced us. Grace pulled him out by the hind legs. His white fur was covered with frost. His eyes remained stubbornly half-open.

"Hello, baby," Grace said to "it." She tried to stand Priceless upright on the table with one hand, her other hand still grasping the portrait of Sean. The dog fell over with a loud knock. I half-expected to see his head snap off. Grace placed the painting of Sean against the cupboards on the floor and sat down on a kitchen chair. She placed the frozen Priceless in her lap so that he seemed to be looking sleepily at me. "Draw us," she commanded. She didn't seem to mind the melted beads of water seeping into her skirt.

"Yes, ma'am," I said. I drew for more than an hour while Grace recited "The Rime of the Ancient Mariner" for me. She knew the whole thing by heart. Pretty amazing, if you ask me. And a little boring too.

When we had both had enough, and Priceless's fur was thawed, she shoved him back into the freezer, and I helped her hang Sean's portrait in her bedroom, which was not cluttered at all but pretty spare-looking. We hung it above a bookcase, where she could see it first thing in the morning and last thing at night. My reward was a handful of chocolate-covered raisins. Grace didn't wash her hands before she gave them to me. I ate them anyway.

When I got back to Libby's, she and Dan were both out on my porch fussing about the screened wall.

"What are you doing?" I asked.

"Measuring," Libby said. "I'm having this room enclosed so that I can use it year-round."

"The insurance man called and told her she was filthy rich." Dan released the spring-steel measuring tape back into its shell.

Libby arched an eyebrow. "Hardly," she said. "But it does open up some options."

I sat down on the bed. "Is this going to be your bedroom, then?" I asked.

Libby sat next to me on the bed looking through the drawings in my notebook. "I don't know," she mused. "Maybe. How are you going to paint Grace now?" she asked.

"Sitting like that in her kitchen, with Priceless on her lap, only his head will be the head of her son, Sean. I thought of it at the beginning of the summer already, but I'm really ready to do it now."

"You like living on the edge, don't you?" Dan smiled.

The phone rang in the kitchen. "I'll get it," I said, and left the two of them sitting on the porch.

"Susan, you were going to call me." It was Mother.

"Oh," I said, looking at my watch. "I'm sorry; I didn't realize it was this late. I've been away all day and all night. I'm sorry," I said again.

"Were you able to get a plane reservation?"

"No," I said. "I forgot all about it."

"Susan! How could you forget?" She sounded steamed. It seemed like people had been mad at me all my life.

"I had to go to work this morning when I wasn't expecting to, and worked all day, and then Grace got back from New York—"

"I'll make the reservation for you," she said, cutting me off. "We need to know when you're coming now or else we can't make any plans. And you've got to get ready for school. I'll make it for this Sunday. That way Libby can drive you to the airport without taking time off from work."

I can take care of myself. Mostly.

"I can call," I said.

"Let me do it," she said. "I'll call you in the morning. I'll arrange it so that you can pick up the ticket at Logan Airport. Okay?"

"Yeah—thanks."

"I'll talk to you tomorrow, honey. Love you."

"Love you too."

Dan was leaving when I hung up the phone. He and Libby murmured to each other at the front door. I felt lethargic and sat down at the kitchen table. If I had wanted to stay, I should have made arrangements. I should have gotten a place, a roommate.

You thought you would marry Willy.

"Your mother?" Libby asked, sitting down across the table from me.

I nodded and tried to smile.

"It's going to storm," she continued. "It's fun to sleep on the porch during a storm."

"Yes." I wondered where Willy would sleep during the storm or if he was even within range of it. It was surprising, now that I thought about the way Willy lived his life, that he had never been hit with a bolt of lightning.

"Mother's making a reservation for Sunday," I said. "Probably in the afternoon."

"Fine," Libby said. Thunder rumbled off in the distance. She leafed lazily through a Pella window catalog.

"Lib?"

"Mmm?" Her finger ran down a listing of prices.

"Was it hard for you to leave home? I mean, were Grandma and Grandpa all right about it? Or did they want you to stay home?"

She looked up. "They wanted me to stay with a capital *S*. I applied to schools in the East on my own, and when I had a scholarship in hand, I told them I was going. They about had a stroke."

"But you left anyway."

"Yes—I was pretty stubborn." The thought of her eighteen-year-old stubborn self made her smile.

"How did you know—I mean, how could you be sure that you were doing the right thing?"

She closed the catalog and laid it aside. "I don't think I thought about right and wrong. I was going to college like they wanted me to. I just didn't want to stay in Utah to do it." She pulled the cotton sweater over her head and plopped it down on the kitchen table. She was always undressing in the kitchen. "But if you want to talk about right and wrong—then, I was right. I knew what I wanted to do and I did it. They wanted the safer alternative for me. But that was their job, don't you see? They were supposed to take care of me and keep me safe. My job was to go away." She yawned. "Eventually all parents and children have to have such a fight, it seems to me." She pulled her belt off and laid it next to the sweater.

"I guess so." I said. She made it sound so normal.

The wind was now blowing the curtain wildly, and Libby moved across the room to shut the window. She turned and leaned back against the sink. "You don't want to go home, do you?" she said, crossing her arms in front of her.

I turned in my chair. "No."

"What *do* you want?"

I told her about the museum school and about staying a year for residency and saving my money. "I want to live in Boston—it's my spiritual home," I said. I thought she would smile at that, but she only sighed and looked down at her feet. "I've wanted that from the beginning," I said.

"So what's wrong with that?"

That surprised me. "Mother doesn't want me to."

"Sue, I don't understand you sometimes. Your mother wouldn't have wanted you dating Willy either, but that didn't stop you. Why does the thought of staying here to go to work and to school make you so helpless?"

A thunderclap seemed to hit the side of the building, it was so loud, and we both started. It began raining.

"I don't know—it's—it's that I don't trust my own judgment anymore."

"Because of Willy?"

I nodded. The rain pelted against the kitchen window, and I could hear the tree branches battering the screen on the back porch.

Libby was half-sitting on the counter now. "Dating Willy was stupid; there's no doubt about that," she said. "You weren't prepared to take him on. You couldn't have been. No one in our family could take on Willy. Forget him."

"I feel ashamed whenever I think of him."

She shoved a chair next to mine and sat on it, leaning forward. "Remember that dream you had last spring? You told me about a dream where you were high up on stilts, and you felt exhilarated and afraid of falling at the same time?"

I nodded, surprised that she remembered.

"Well, you've fallen off the stilts. You've fallen flat on your face. This is it—you're on the asphalt right now. This is as bad as it gets. It's not that bad, you see. I mean, it really isn't. Now that you know that, get back on the stilts and get on with things."

I couldn't help but smile at her.

"Do I sound like one of those high school counselors?" She laughed.

"I don't know; I never had to visit one."

"Well, my lips are tired of flapping," she said. The rain fell steadily against the window behind her. "You can stay here, Sue, if you want." She was removing her skirt as she said this.

"I can?" I had thought she was ecstatic to get rid of me.

"Of course."

"Even after everything with Willy and the horrendous phone bill—oh, I have that money in my purse, by the way." I leapt up to get my purse from the porch, but she pushed me back down into the chair.

"I believe you." She laughed.

"I thought you were mad at me."

"I was—still am occasionally when I look around my bare apartment, but"—she shrugged—"so we had a fight. I can stand it. Can you?"

I began to feel tremendously light and porous and giddy and afraid all at once. "I thought I knew everything about Willy," I said. "But then nothing worked out the way I thought it would. I thought I was right and everyone else was wrong. And it turned out that I was wrong and everyone else was right. I'm not sure I know what I should do anymore."

"What you want for yourself hasn't changed, has it?"

"I want to paint."

"Is that so wrong?"

"I want to live in Boston," I said.

"So what's wrong with that?"

"You're serious—I can stay here a little longer?"

"Absolutely. I like you. Dan likes you. The porch should be finished before fall sets in, so there's room for you, but"—she grew serious—"you have to go home and work things out with your parents. After that you are welcome to come back and stay in that very room." She pointed to the porch.

"That's what I want to do," I said. "That's exactly what I want to do."

＄

Springville, Utah 84663

＄

It was the sweet peas that finally made me cry. Mother had planted them along the chain-link fence surrounding our backyard. Maybe it was the frilled pink-and-violet blossoms, delicate and fragile—the way I felt—reminding me how far away from Boston, from the Bijou Theater, from Libby and Dan and from Grace I really was that made me sad. Maybe it was that I was sitting on the grass, my back leaning against the cherry tree that linked me to the Willy of ten years before. Maybe it was seeing the new lacy curtains in Marianne's basement window, reminding me that Ellen Turley lived there now. The hated sign in the front window of the basement, HAIRSTYLING BY MARIANNE, was gone. I missed it terribly and I cried.

Maybe also it was that I had been home over a week and had not said what I needed to say. Mother talked about my going to college with such excitement. She and Fiona shared the same intensity about it. I felt like an outsider and a fraud. To tell Mother I was postponing it a year and returning to Boston would hurt her. Not to tell her would crush me. That very afternoon I had been working on my painting of Grace, Priceless, and Sean. Mother walked past my bedroom door, which was open so that the cool air could circulate.

"Who's that you're painting?" she asked, stopping in the doorway.

"Grace McGregor," I said. "She lives next door to Libby."

"The woman who was on *David Letterman*?"

"Yes."

"Is that a dog or a child she's holding?" She leaned her head through the doorway to have a better look.

I kept my voice soft: "It's her son's head on the body of her pet dog." I kept painting.

There was a moment of shocked recognition. "Susan," she gasped. "What's she going to think when she sees that? You've just got to stop—"

I cut her off: "Mother," I snapped, "you cannot dictate how I will paint!" My voice brimmed with hot conviction.

"Well, excuse me," she said, and disappeared down the hall.

From my easel I saw Thomas's letters with the fish and wild-flowers strewn along the margins tacked to the wall. Mother would like fish and wildflowers. My painting hurt her. I cried.

The mountains shimmered in the rich pink light of twilight. I saw them through tears. Through tears I saw Mother's face in the glass of the kitchen window. Our eyes held across the space of the backyard. And then she was gone. I cried.

I cried while she walked through the gate, across the lawn, and sat down beside me, her back resting against the trunk of the cherry tree, her shoulder touching mine. She said nothing for quite a while but let me cry. Finally she cleared her throat a little and said, "I noticed that you didn't bring any of your paintings home." Her hand patted down the grass between us. "I have a feeling that it's a sign of some kind." Her head turned to me. "A sign I've been ignoring."

I nodded and sobbed into her shoulder.

"Tell me," she said. "I'm ready to listen."

"I don't want to go to school here," I blurted out. "I want to go back to Boston."

She sighed heavily, and a little *mmm* escaped her lips.

"I want to go to the museum school of the Boston Museum of Fine Arts next year after I've established residency."

"Art school?" Mother said.

"Yes."

"Would you live with Libby?"

I nodded. "She's having the porch converted into a second bedroom." I cried afresh to think of the long windows, ready for installment, that had arrived the day before I came home.

Mother put my arm through hers and rubbed it gently. "Why did you come home at all? I mean, why didn't you just call and tell us?"

"I was afraid you'd be mad, and—"

"And?"

"And I didn't want you to be disappointed, and—"

"And?"

I convulsed into sobs. "I've been really stupid." I gasped. "Willy."

Mother's body grew rigid. "Willy?" she asked.

"I-I met Willy in Boston." I struggled between gasps to speak.

"Willy Gerard?"

"Y-yes." I kept my head buried in her shoulder.

"You *saw* Willy?"

"A lot of times. I was so stupid!"

"Willy," she breathed. "I wondered why you weren't wearing the armadillo necklace anymore."

"He took it!" I said, choking back the sobs. "He took it from me —said he would make a bracelet to match, but he was just stealing it back to sell it! He just wanted to sell it!" I sobbed freely. I didn't care what I sounded like, what I looked like. I held on to my mother.

"You saw Willy?" She was still getting used to the idea of Willy appearing after all these years.

"All summer long," I said. I told her about forcing Salvatore to make a movie pass for him. "He came to the theater all summer long, and I paid for his tickets. I paid for every stinking movie he came to." I told her about the concert, about the Isabella Stewart Gardner Museum, about my birthday. "I thought we would get married! Can you believe how stupid I was?" I bawled some more. "And he stole everything in sight. He stole Libby's carpets, her cameras, her antiques, and my paintings—all my paintings—everything I'd brought with me and everything I'd worked on during the summer. He took everything!" I was out of breath.

"And your confidence," she finished.

I rested my head in her lap now while she stroked my head. It was almost dark. "I love the mountains with the black light on them," she said. "That's what your father and I used to call it when you were little—a black light on the mountains."

I pulled away and looked into her face. "*You* called it a black light? I always thought it was Willy who said that. I was sure of it."

"I don't think Willy noticed the mountains very much." She pulled me close to her again. "He couldn't sell *them*."

It made me laugh to think of Willy trying to pawn the Rocky Mountains. I could barely see the sweet peas along the fence, although their fragrance filled the yard. "The whole thing with Willy—it scared me," I said finally. "I mean, I was so sure I was right about everything—so sure that you and everyone else were wrong about Willy. I was the right one, not you. But I wasn't, don't you see? I was totally and absurdly wrong about him. It makes me ill to think about it. It makes me literally ill. How do I know if I'm right about things? I had this dream . . ." I told her about the dream of being up on the stilts, of the exhilaration and the anxiety. "Dreams tell the future," I said. "I fell flat on my face on the asphalt."

"Well"—she sighed—"you did sort of splatter there at the end." She rubbed my arms, which were beginning to get goose bumps now that the sun was completely gone behind the mountains. "I doubt that you'll splatter that badly again."

"That's what Libby said."

She smiled.

"I don't use the silent five anymore. It seemed kind of dumb once I got to Boston."

Mother laughed quietly. She hummed a little and then stopped. "I'm not the best person to understand what you're about," she said. "I know that."

That made me cry all over again.

"But there are plenty of other people—kind people—who are willing to help you get the kind of life you want. I wouldn't ignore them too long." She pushed me gently away and wiped her own eyes with her hand. "We'd better go in," she said. "It feels more like fall than summer out here after the sun's gone down." She pushed a stray piece of hair away from my forehead.

Derriere came to the window and yelled out in his shrillest voice, "Mom, is Susan here? Mom?"

"I'm here," I called back.

"The telephone's for you. Hurry up, I've got to call Spencer!"

"Who is it?" I yelled to him.

"It's a funny name. Food! Thomas Food."

"Thomas Roode," I corrected him. "He's back from Italy." I jumped up and ran across the lawn and then turned back when I reached the gate.

"I love you," I said to the dark form still sitting under the cherry tree.

"I love you too," she said.

About the Author

Louise Plummer lives in Provo, Utah, where she teaches writing. She and her husband, Tom, have four sons: Jonathan, Edmund, Charles, and Samuel. She has a master's degree in English from the University of Minnesota.

Her first novel, *The Romantic Obsessions and Humiliations of Annie Sehlmeier,* won Honorable Mention in the Third Annual Delacorte Press Prize for an Outstanding First Young Adult Novel contest. This novel, *My Name Is Sus5an Smith. The 5 Is Silent.,* won first prize for a young adult novel in the 1989 Utah Arts Council Creative Writing Competition.